THE DAY OF DARKNESS

BOOK 6

DEMIGODS ACADEMY

THE DAY OF DARKNESS

ELISA S. AMORE

KIERA LEGEND

CHAPTER ONE

MELANY

*a*s I walked over the stone floor of the Fates' stark granite cave, searching the space for any sign of Zeus's thread of life, the enormity of what I had hidden inside my pocket seemed to weigh me down. Lifting my leg and taking a step forward without shaking with anxiousness and excitement, was a significant achievement. I wondered if the others could see my struggle, because I felt like it was evident in the lines of my face.

I hoped they didn't. Guilt pressed heavily against my chest already for dragging them here on another one of my perilous, and possibly, overly righteous quests. How many times had I put my best friends, those closest to me, in danger? Too many to count.

This time was no different.

We'd broken into Hera's Hall. Had been teleported to a barren land with no clear path, and now we were in an odd mountain's cave in the middle of nowhere, looking for a needle in a haystack—or rather, a particular thread in a giant woven blanket. It was an impossible task, but I was dead set on completing it at any cost.

I paused and glanced at Lucian, who was upside down on the cave ceiling, inspecting threads. His attention was firmly affixed to his task, concentration written on his features. Jasmine was huddled with Mia along one wall, consoling her girlfriend. Mia still looked pale and nauseated, not used to the strange and dangerous situations that we always seemed to get into. I felt bad for her as I noted the clammy sweat that sheened her skin.

Frown lines etched deep on Georgina's brow while she crouched by the spinning wheel, inspecting the structure and its complex mechanics.

Cassandra was the closest to me, and I could see her picking up individual threads, reading them, then gently setting them back down where they'd been. She surprised me the most, on how instantly she fit into our motley crew. Although, I suspected it had a lot to do with how she felt about Lucian. Even now, she stole glances at him, hoping no one noticed. I wasn't going to bring it up. I knew she'd be mortified that I had most certainly took notice.

Everyone seemed to be concentrating on what needed to be done, and not at all concerned with me. So, it weren't my friends who were holding me back, but rather the burden of my conscience that was weighing me down.

Straightening, I shook off the feeling. I'd deal with it later, when I had time to poke into those nooks and crannies of my soul.

Having tucked the guilt away, I continued to sweep the floor for any sign of Zeus's lifeline. If we could find it, then there wouldn't be the threat of anyone trying to resurrect him. Although, I still needed to find out who that particular person was. Whoever it ended up being, was an enemy.

Despite that, there was still the matter of Death taking a holiday and the dead not dying, oh, and the Fates' disappearance. At least, that would be the biggest issue we'd had to deal with, and we could figure out a way to fix the other things without the portent of Zeus's thunderous return crushing down upon our well-meaning heads.

I knew that if the God returned, his first order of business would be to kill me, followed quickly by everyone I loved and cared about, which would be everyone in this cave. Also, I imagined every God, Goddess, and Demigod that helped me along the way—Hephaistos, Demeter, Dionysus, Heracles, Charon, the Furies, and Chiron, all came to mind —would pay in some way. If not by true death, then by some other horrible and twisted fate, which could make death seem preferable.

Being locked in Tartarus would be one of them.

I swallowed thickly at the thought. His spite was legendary, literally a part of historical record, so I imagined he'd strike down my friends first while forcing me to watch. The mere thought of it made me shudder. I could handle my own torture—I'd been there, done that—but I didn't think I could resist watching those I cared about being hurt.

Surely, I'd lose my shit.

No. I wouldn't let that happen. No matter what. I couldn't.

. . .

After another long hour, or so, of looking at thousands upon thousands of threads, the heft of our task seemed insurmountable. I was ready to give up and go back to the academy, to take a step back, to try and find another way to stop Zeus's resurrection. Yet, I knew that a lot of it came from the fact that I had what I ultimately desired in the front pocket of my pants—Hades's lifeline.

It was everything I'd been dreaming about for months. It was all I wanted. To have him back at my side, in any way. So, I kept my mouth shut. If the others ever found out... I didn't want to even consider how angry and disappointed they would be with me. Especially Lucian. It would crush him, and I didn't want to hurt him anymore than I already had.

The picture of his face if he discovered my betrayal formed in my mind's eye. The shock at my duplicity shadowed deep in his eyes. I didn't like the mental image, so I forced it away. Locked it down deeply.

He deserved so much more than a girl like me.

"Hey! I think I found it."

My head swung around to see Lucian on the opposite side of the cave, standing perpendicular on the wall, his soft golden waves hanging over his face.

Seeing that the laws of physics didn't work here was still baffling, and a bit stomach clenching. It tinted the entire quest with a shadow of disbelief. As though I was dreaming, knew I was dreaming, but couldn't force myself to awake.

I pushed the feeling away, shaking it off like I always did, and put my focus onto where Lucian pointed, his finger indicating to the stone floor.

There was a slight glint, something shiny reflecting off the light emanating from the globes of fire we lit around the cavern. All the threads were woven from gold, but this particular one shone just a bit brighter. Like it was a more pure form of gold, a more valuable one. Like Hades's lifeline, this one possessed some power even after being severed.

A lot of power, actually. Now that I set my gaze on it, I could feel it. The sheer energy radiating from it was astounding.

We all moved toward that spot, eager to retrieve it and get out of there. Georgina arrived first, but as she reached for the thread, the entire cave started to rumble and shake. She hadn't even brushed it with her fingers, so it couldn't be the lifeline, could it? Whatever it was, it felt like an earthquake. Just what we needed while deep inside of a cave.

Bits of rock fell from the ceiling and smashed

onto the floor. One big chunk, a razor-sharp stalactite—nearly the size of my body—came crashing down, almost hitting me. Thank the Gods, I managed to jump out of the way before it could slice into my skull.

"Get out of the open!" I shouted to the others as I moved quickly across the space. I waved my arms to demonstrate what I meant. "Press up against the walls!"

Everyone followed suit just as the ground beneath us shook even more. I could feel the vibrations rattling through my bones. Ren fell to his knees, one leg hitting a large shard of stone and bending unnaturally. A cry of pain erupted from his throat.I ran to him, helping him up, and hauling him over to the wall as quickly as we could. I spotted a trail of scarlet blood following us. Ren must've torn open his pants and his knee on the razor-sharp rock.

I pressed up against the far wall again, not far from where Jasmine and Mia were, feeling the cold stone against my back. In sickening shock, I watched as the ground started to undulate, creaking before cracking open.

It wasn't like what I'd seen during the battle of Pecunia, when the ground spilt apart, creating the chasm into which Revana fell to her death. No, this looked like something was drilling its way up through the earth. Crumbs of soil, chunks of gravel, and shards of rock showered down around us.

Pieces of stone and dirt piled up on top on the sides until there was a large gaping hole in the cave. Given the loud rattling sound coming from below, I suspected that something big was coming up through it. I was scared to peer down into the hole, but I did it anyway, tension stiffening my limbs.

Bad idea. What I saw made my guts churn over.

The eyeless bone-white face of what looked like a gaunt, gigantic worm, came charging from the hole. When it emerged, its massive mouth opened to make a strange, skin crawling sound, much like a growl. The way its body undulated was mesmer-izing in a strange way. Goose flesh rose all over my body, and a shiver rushed up my spine. Its gaping maw was lined with tiny sharp teeth and wriggling cilia-like protrusions.

Mia's scream echoed around us, and the beast's flanges swayed in her direction. Its head swiveled too, focusing deep black holes on her.

That was not good.

Considering the hideous creature didn't have

eyes, I figured it sensed where we were by sound, using the grotesque looking cilia in its mouth. Jasmine must've figured that out too, because she slapped a hand over Mia's mouth, and then moved them to another part of the cave. Their movements were exaggerated, as though they were walking in slow motion even though they were hurrying, and I realized it was because they were trying to be as quiet as they could, getting themselves out of harm's way before the beast could strike.

And strike it did.

Like a deadly, venomous viper, it lunged to where Jasmine and Mia had just been standing, its mouth wide and ready to inhale whatever it found. With deadly power and force, the monster crashed against the spot, its mouth moving hungrily. Luckily, it found nothing but stone and dirt, and the unfortunate, severed golden strands of life. Like a living vacuum, it sucked it all down. The sound it made as it fed caused nausea to roil in my gut, though I almost hoped that one of those threads belonged to Zeus. Then it would be gone forever, down into the belly of the gauntly beast.

Snapping out of the shock, I realized we needed to get out of the cave and into the tunnel as fast and as quietly as we could, since the beast seemed to hunt through sound.

I couldn't yell across the room to warn the others like I wanted to, so I swallowed my words, and took a tiny step away from the wall I'd been pressed into. Lifting my arms, I waved back and forth to get their attention, hoping that the sound of my limbs moving through the air was faint. Luckily, the creature didn't seem to pick up on it, so I kept waving. Once everyone was looking at me, I motioned toward the entrance to the tunnel we'd come through with exaggerated movements.

Lucian's short nod was the first answer I received, he was propping Ren up against him because our friend was clearly in a lot of pain. Jasmine and Mia had clasped hands tightly, and were already inching their way over to the tunnel. Mia looked like she was in shock, but at least she was walking.

Cassandra, on the other hand, was frozen in place, still pressed against a wall nearby. I waved at her again, and she just looked back at me with glassy eyes. I wasn't sure what it would take to get her to snap out of it. I might have to go grab her and move her myself.

Glancing across the room to Georgina, my

mouth went dry. I knew she'd seen my gesture toward the tunnel, but her focus was on the heaving ground and on Zeus's thread. The gleaming gold strand had shifted a bit when the white worm burrowed its way through the rock, but for some reason, it hadn't been sucked down into the creature's massive, amorphous body.

I wanted to yell at her that it wasn't worth the risk, but it actually kind of was. And I had a feeling that she wouldn't listen to me anyway.

While the others made their way to the tunnel as silently as possible, and with slow motion style movements, I thought about ways to distract the worm so Georgina could get Zeus's thread and still make it out of there alive. It was clear she'd made up her mind. I decided to get closer to it, which on first thought seemed like an insane idea, but I had to do something, or she was going to get herself killed trying to get the stupid lifeline.

The worm's big tube head swung around toward me when my feet slid on the shifting rocks. My boot hit a small pebble, sending it rolling across the rocky floor. It opened its mouth to "smell" or "hear" me, I couldn't decipher which sense it was using. I supposed it didn't matter, as long as we got away from it.

Out of the corner of my eye, I spied Georgina reaching for the thread with her good arm, her fingers brushing over it. I tensed, praying that she would be able to grab it. Maybe we could all get out of this without having to fight some beast to the death for once. Finally, her hand grasped it, and she straightened, holding it up for me to see. A grin illuminated her face at her triumph.

I returned her smile, and the tension capturing my body relaxed a little.

Then everything changed, yet again.

The ground was still shaking from the worm beast breaking through, but it suddenly began to rock even harder. I struggled to keep my balance, falling painfully to my knees before dragging myself back up—no easy feat with the massive tremors that were rocking the cave. I'd barely swallowed a shout when another worm burst through the rock... near Georgina.

I hadn't even heard it coming.

She turned toward it, moving as if in slow motion, just as its wide slit of a mouth opened, revealing the undulating cilia inside.

"No!" I screamed, springing into action. My feet dashed past the first monster, muscles burnings, a fireball forming in the palm of my hand.

The first worm somehow followed my movements and twisted toward me, seeking me as its target. It sliced through the crisp cave air like a leather whip, smashing into the rock wall beside me, and chunks from the roof rained down where it had hit. As it retreated, gearing up for a second strike, I turned and flung a ball of fire into its mouth, the flame sputtering slightly in the damp air. I watched the blaze get swallowed by the dark depths of the creature's throat.

The shriek that emanated from it rattled the entire cave, shooting a bolt of pain into my ears, which started to ring over and over again. Grimacing from the reverberating ache inside my head, I kept moving, one foot in front of the other, just as sparks erupted between my fingers. I was no longer scared, the fear replaced by rage.

I was going to fry that fucker.

The others flew into action, a flurry of movement happening around me—we were long past the point of escaping stealthily. More unholy, ululating shrieks from the creatures split the air, flashes of bright fire erupting when my friends joined me, mounting an attack on the beast that was doing its best to swallow me whole.

All I could focus on though, was the second

beast looming over Georgina with its gaping maw wide open. It was huge—at least six feet in diameter — bigger than the other white worm, and faster, which was surprising, especially for such a slumberous looking creature. The blood drained from my face, and my heart leapt into my throat as I watched it strike; she ran from it, but the monster got closer and closer to her with every blow.

There was nothing I could do.

I knew its next attack would succeed, and a scream tore unbidden from my throat. Leaving my friends to handle my worm, I leapt across the cave, arms outstretched, fire ball in hand... but I was too slow. The beast lunged again; its lightning quick movements barely visible to the naked eye.

My knees crashed roughly on the earth; my mouth open in a silent scream as the monster snatched Georgina.

It devoured her in one big gulp.

A slight sound of satisfaction echoed from its depths, like a pleased humming while it swallowed her. Sickened, we all watched the white worm retreat into its hole, taking my best friend with it.

CHAPTER TWO

LUCIAN

One minute Georgina was there, and the next she wasn't…

Shock washed over me, rooting me in place. I couldn't believe what had just happened. I was barely aware of anything other than the fact that Georgina was gone, but I did notice the first worm also retracted into its hole. We'd done some damage to it, but obviously not enough to kill it and it was escaping, going down into the bowls of the earth.

"Don't shoot lightning! It will bounce off the walls!" I shouted at Melany as she flew over to the second hole, where the larger worm had disappeared. Her hands sparked with the unbridled rage I was certain she held inside. I felt sick to my stomach, and I knew that our friends all did, too.

It was too late though. I winced, ducking at what I knew was about to come. She'd already flung her hands toward the split rock floor, aiming her deadly fire at the worm-like beast that had already escaped.

Bright white, jagged, fiery bolts bounced off the hole's walls and shot to the right—where Ren and I had been huddled. Whatever his injury was, it was enough to hinder his movement, so I had to push him out of the way not to be fried by Melany's fire.

A ragged grunt left Ren's throat when his knee unavoidably hit the floor again. More blood stained his pants from the sudden impact, a sticky crimson pool forming below us. We hadn't had time to tie off his injury.

The fire reverberated around the cave, and I noticed another white-hot bolt zipping toward Cassandra.

I reacted.

Flying across the cave, I quickly unfurled my wings, yet kept them close to my body for maximum velocity. I managed to get in front of her before the lightning struck her in the chest and burned a hole right through her. The electricity hit my abdomen like a punch and sizzled all over my skin. It hurt. It hurt like acid had been poured over my skin, but I concentrated on absorbing it into my body. Instead of burning, my skin turned bright red, irritated and raw.

It looked like having a really bad sunburn. Felt like it too.

"Are you okay?" I looked Cassandra from head to toe, making sure no errant lightning had gone around me to sear her body.

Eyes wide, she shook her head. She looked pale and shaky. "You saved me." Her voice sounded so surprised that it startled me.

I didn't get a chance to respond, because I had to run over to the worm hole to stop Melany from diving into it headfirst.

"Let me go!" She pulled out of my grasp, glaring daggers at me. I grabbed for her again, absorbing the fiery sparks shooting along her skin. She wasn't scared, she was full of rage.

"You can't just go in there, Mel." I had to say it, even though I knew she wasn't in a place to listen to reason.

"It took Gina. Of course I'm going in after it.

Standing here, talking about it, is wasting valuable time she doesn't have!"

"Okay, but let's make a plan. Let's do it together."

Melany looked like she might argue, but I gradually felt her muscles relax, just enough that I was sure she wasn't about to dive in alone.

The others joined us at the hole; Jasmine had helped Ren over. He slumped down onto the floor, resting his back against the stone wall. Sweat popped up on his brow and upper lip, leaving a greasy sheen on his skin. He didn't look too good.

Before I could ask someone to help him, Cassandra crouched next to him and inspected his injury. He started to pull away, to say he was fine, but she quelled him with a look that said she meant business. I didn't know if she had strong healing abilities, but with the way her hands fluttered over the huge gash on his knee, her movements competent and sure, I suspected she knew what she was doing.

We watched keenly as she ripped off a piece of her shirt to wrap around the gaping wound. It probably wasn't the most sterile dressing, given that we'd all been tossed around the cave like marbles in a jar, but I supposed it was better than nothing.

Pulling my attention away from Ren and Cassandra, I grabbed a rope that had been lying on the ground and brought it back to Melany. I moved quickly so that she didn't have a chance to grow impatient and do something rash, like going after the beast alone.

"We can tie this around your waist," I suggested, ignoring the scathing look she gave me. "Just in case we have to yank you back."

"I'm not coming back until I have Gina."

I thought about reasoning with her, but the determined glare in her eyes told me it would be pointless. Never mind that I knew her, and was certain she was going to do what she wanted anyway. Really, I didn't blame her. This was Georgina we were talking about. Not only was she Melany's best friend, she was the best and brightest of us all.

Sighing, I looked at the others. "So, what do we got? Giant white worms that can't see but use their other senses. Strong, fast, and live underground. It's not ringing a bell for me. Anyone else heard of these creatures before?"

Mia's nose scrunched up as she considered it. "I'm pretty sure Artemis mentioned them in one of her classes."

"Anything you can remember would be help-ful," Melany added as she inspected the worm hole in the wall, getting ready to get inside it. Impatience was etched in every line of her body. "Especially of ways to kill them."

"I remember her saying that they are usually peaceful creatures." Mia bit her lower lip in concen-tration while the rest of us shot her a look of disbelief.

"Obviously not," Melany growled, balling her hands into tight fists.

"They're supposedly not carnivorous," Mia added. Her voice wavered a bit under our stares, then strengthened. I believed her—believed that this was what she had been told, anyway.

"Why did they have big teeth then?" Melany pressed, agitated.

Mia shrugged, but lifted her chin in the air. "To chew plants and grass."

"Are you sure that's what Artemis said?" I interjected.

Mia nodded.

"Why did it swallow Gina then? If not for food?"

"Maybe they didn't come on their own?" Mia suggested. "I mean, this mountain, this cave doesn't seem like a normal place for worms to be. Wouldn't they be in an area with a lot of dirt, grass, and hills?"

"I think Mia is right," I agreed, seeing Melany begin to bounce on the balls of her feet with impatience.

"Doesn't matter right now. All that matters is how I'm going to slice it open and get Gina back." Melany unsheathed the dagger she always carried on her belt while I eyed it curiously. I couldn't help myself. I knew it was something she picked up in the underworld, and I always wondered if it had been a gift from Hades.

My jaw tensed but I pushed that jealous thought away. I *was* jealous, yet this was not the time or place to be petty.

When she gestured toward the hole, I nodded. My hand reached for hers, feeling her pulse beat against my palm. "Be careful. Remember we're here for you. We can pull you back."

"I know," she whispered, squeezing my hand in return, and I felt my skin heat beneath her touch.

Jasmine picked up a chunk of rock, holding it tightly until it glowed red. After cutting a piece of rope, she tied it around the rock, fashioning a necklace that emitted a soft red luminescence. Solemnly, she draped it over Melany's head.

"It should give you some light without burning you."

"Thank you." Melany nodded briskly to Jasmine, and faced me again.

Making a cradle out of my hands, I lowered them for her to place her foot, and lifted her into the hole; it was just wide enough that she could stand in it but the top of her head would most definitely brush against the rock Without hesitation, Melany ran into the hole,as fast as she could to save our friend.

MELANY

It got dark rather quickly inside the wormhole, as I followed it deep into the rock of the mountain. The soft red glow from the stone Jasmine gave me only illuminated about a foot in front of me, but I was thankful for it. I considered igniting my hands with flames, but I was already juggling a dagger and my anger, I didn't need something else to distract me.

My gut churned with guilt while I jogged through the tunnel, making me sick. I should've dove into the hole immediately, no matter what Lucian said. Those precious few minutes might've been the difference between finding Georgina dead or alive. The mere thought made me wince.

Although Mia said the creatures didn't eat meat, I couldn't rely on that. I resented the time Lucian took from me to tie a rope around my waist. I knew I shouldn't but I did, and there was no point in denying it while being here, alone and in the dark, with only my own thoughts to keep me company. I was feeling resentful around him a lot lately.

I didn't know how far ahead of me the worm was, but thankfully, I could still hear it squirming through the hole. Its slimy sides made a sticky sound as it moved. I could also feel the vibrations of it along the jagged walls of the tunnel while it burrowed ever deeper into the earth. It was unsettling to know I could run into it at any moment, and it was difficult to keep my quick pace with my muscles tense, awaiting the shock and surprise.

At least it still afforded me an opportunity to save Georgina. I'd go through any horror to have that chance.

Increasing my pace, the jagged stone above me

scraped against my head. I was sure to have a few cuts and bumps along the way.. The slight sting I felt radiating over my skull and down my neck was nothing compared to the horror Georgina must've been experiencing in the belly of the beast. I wanted to scream to her to hold on, tell her I was coming for her.

Hopefully she trusted me enough that she already knew.

Desperate, I kept pushing myself to go faster, until I spotted something ahead—just at the very edge of the faint crimson glow from my rock. It was the worm. It roared when it sensed my presence, and the vibration from its outrage caused bits of rock to crumble from the roof. Pieces of stone peppered my face, dust getting into my eyes, but I didn't slow down.

No matter how fast I moved, the creature moved faster. It felt like, rather than me getting closer to it, the beast was slithering further and further away. Determined to slow the creature down, I stopped for a moment to form a ball of fire in my hand. Sucking in a deep breath, I let it fly toward it. It was impossible for me to miss in this tunnel. There was nowhere to go to dodge it. I was rewarded with a shriek as the flames splattered over its head.

Then I heard a sound that nearly made me weep...

"Help me!"

It was Georgina. She was still alive inside the gullet of the worm. Thank the Gods.

"Gina! I'm coming. Don't give up!!"

"Mel! Oh, my Gods, Mel!" Her voice was more frantic than I'd ever heard it, which was saying something, considering all of the quests that I'd dragged her on in the past.

I would save her. As far as I was concerned, there was no other option. Still, tears erupted from my eyes as I continued to run, fighting my way through the earth. "Fight it from the inside, Gina!"

Her response never reached me. The tunnel suddenly began to tremble, and the walls around me crumbled, forcing me down to my knees and burying me in the rubble.

Dirt and rock pelted me in the head and face. I gasped, then coughed as I inhaled a cloud of dust. Soon, my arms and legs were pinned to the floor below me and I couldn't move. Careful not to become completely suffocated, I stopped struggling against the barrage of rocks, and took a deep breath. I feared it might be the last of my oxygen, so I concentrated on the earth and stones around me. I still had earth powers, the ones that Georgina gifted me during the battle against Zeus, so I called on them to help me out of this situation before the debris stole my breath.

Focusing on the debris surrounding me, I asked it to move away, willing my energy, my powers, to move from my body to the stone. It was slow at first, excruciatingly so, and I thought maybe it wouldn't obey me, but then the gravel around me started to vibrate. I focused harder and little pieces of rock rolled back into the walls.

After a few seconds I sucked in a huge breath, able to breathe a bit easier and shuffle my arms and legs. They weren't so constricted anymore. Suddenly, I felt the tug of the rope on my waist. I must've moved enough of the earth for the others to be able to yank me out of the hole.

"No!" I shouted, trying to dig my elbows and knees into the gravel, to stay where I was.

I didn't want to be pulled out again. I wanted to go further in, because that was where Georgina was. Still, I could feel the tension in the cord around my body increasing. At first, the tugging was hesitant, but soon I was yanked backward hard and fast, until I popped out of the hole and nearly fell onto the ground.

Lucian was there, hands under my arms, holding me secure.

"Are you okay?" He brushed off the dust and bits of stone from my face and hair. "I didn't think we were going to be able to get you out of there."

"I saw the worm. I heard Gina. She's still alive."

"You heard her from within the worm? Gods!" Jasmine swallowed, her face turning ashen.

Mia nodded. That matched what she knew about the creatures. "Seems logical, if they aren't carnivores. Maybe they're taking her to their lair."

That did not sound good.

"For what purpose?" Lucian asked. "It makes no sense."

"Any mention of where this lair is?" I hissed when Lucian inspected the cuts on my hands. "They're fine." I pulled away. We were wasting valuable time here with superficial things.

I glanced at Ren. He hadn't moved from his spot on the ground. He definitely didn't look well, and it surprised me. He was usually so robust. The gash on his knee must've been more serious than I assumed if it was still keeping him down, even after Cassandra's first aid.

Mia shook her head, hesitant. "I don't remember if she said."

"Okay, well, we need to get the hell out of here and back to the academy. The more time we waste, the less time Gina has." Before I headed for the exit tunnel, I crouched next to Ren and saw that his leg had been splinted while I'd been gone..

"His shin is broken," Lucian explained. "He really twisted it when he fell."

"What did you use?" I looked around, and my gaze landed on a bunch of broken wood that had been the spinning wheel. My heart sunk into my stomach even as the blood drained from my face. I felt nauseous.

"It was the only thing we could use." Lucian's hand settled on my shoulder.

I looked up at him and nodded.

The look he gave me made me think that he possibly knew what I had hidden in my pocket, and that he knew the agony I was feeling at seeing he had destroyed the one instrument that might be able to return the thing I desired the most. Hades.

CHAPTER THREE

MELANY

*W*ithout any further discussion, we got back into the tunnel and left the cave. Once out, we took to the sky. Ren couldn't fly as high as the rest of us because of the extra weight of the wood on his leg, but he still kept up, though I could see that it cost him.

In formation, we flew back to the portal so we could return to the academy. The second I got back, I was going to track down Artemis and find out where the white worms' lair was. She had to know. Georgina may still be alive, but I didn't know for how long. If someone forced those worms to come, then it was to stop us from getting Zeus's thread, and Georgina—who had the thread —was stuck inside a giant beast. I couldn't imagine the horror she was going through in there.

For what seemed like hours, we flew, stopping once to drink from the canteens. I suspected most of us would have pressed on without the break, but it was easy to see that Ren needed it. I was sure that we should've reached the portal by now, but everything looked the same.

Desolate desert for miles in every direction. Endless rolling dunes of white sand.

If it hadn't been for the one lone shrub that I knew we passed going to the cave, I would've considered that we'd been traveling in the wrong direction.

After another excruciatingly long hour, I pointed to the ground, suggesting for everyone to land.

"I'm pretty sure the portal is gone." Dragging my sweaty hair from my brow, I waved a hand toward the nothingness before us.

Lucian's gaze surveyed the land around us, then turned in the direction we had come. "Yeah, I didn't think we were that far from the cave. A few hours, but it feels like we've been going for a lot longer than that."

"What are we going to do?" Jasmine asked.

Frustration grated my nerve endings. We didn't have time to get stuck here indefinitely. We needed to get back to Gina. I felt like screaming, and almost did before Lucian stepped forward.

"I say we go back to the mountain the cave was in. Maybe there's something else there."

Relieved at a viable option, I nodded. "That's better than flying around out here."

"What if we don't find another way home?" Reaching for Jasmine's hand, Mia held it tightly, showing us the fear and uncertainty growing inside her.

I didn't blame her, but I wasn't giving up yet. I'd escaped from Oblivion; I would find a way out of this barren place.

"We will," Lucian assured.

The hours seemed endless as we flew back to the mountain.

We kept an eye on Ren, not sure that he would be able to make it with his injury. Thankfully, he did. Instead of going into the cave, I did a quick recon along the area and found an oasis on the opposite side.

There was a vibrant green glade next to a sapphire blue pool filled by a stunning waterfall. There were flowers in bright red, pink and purple, and lots of plants growing along the rocky shore. It was a shock to find something like this in the middle of absolute desolation, but very much needed.

Returning to the others, I told them about the refuge I'd spotted. There were a lot of sighs of relief to go around. Our group was strong, but after battling the worms and so many hours of flying, even we needed to rest. We took to the air and flew to the other side of the mountain, giving it one final push before we swooped down to land on the lush green meadow.

Lucian helped Ren settle near the shore of the pool of water, up against an outcropping of moss-covered rocks. Jasmine and Mia immediately went to the water, to test it, and fill up the canteens. Meandering along the shore, Cassandra went to a copse of large trees, returning a few moments later with an armful of golden apples. She gave one to each of us. I gladly bit into it, finishing it in four bites and nearly eating the core. I was so famished. The others did the same.

At least we wouldn't starve to death in this place. Thank the Gods for small graces.

With basic needs sated for the moment, I took to pacing near the pool, going over all our options. Trying to figure out how the hell to get back to the academy to find Georgina. I refused to believe she was beyond saving.

"There have to be other portals out of here." I gestured to the waterfall. "I wonder what's behind the falls."

"Mel, let's just take a breather for a minute. Think things through," Lucian pleaded.

"Gina doesn't have time for us to have a breather." Again, I found my irritation directed at Lucian. It might not be fair, but it was how I was feeling.

With a heavy sigh, Lucian shook his head, pointing to Ren. "He needs attention. At least, let's see if we can get his bleeding to stop."

Guilt rushed through me. Of course, Ren needed medical attention. A quick glance showed me that so much flying hadn't helped him. I was thinking about him too as I pushed for us to find a portal. It would mean he could go to the infirmary and get healed by Chiron.

Walking to Ren's side, I crouched to check his injury. Cassandra had put a good dressing on his knee, but it was fully soaked. He'd lost a lot of blood. Carefully unwrapping the piece of cotton she'd secured, I immediately saw the seriousness of his wound.

It still seeped blood, but the skin around the gash was red. When I touched it he winced, and I could feel the heat radiating from it. There was some infection in the wound, something that had been caused by the beast. He was radiating heat but shivering, his skin pale. Ren definitely had a fever, brought on by the contamination.

If Gina was here, she'd know exactly what plant to look for to bring down his temperature, and to combat the infection. Despite the earth powers coursing through my veins, my knowledge about medicinal herbs was limited. I was hesitant to even try, for fear that I would give him something that would make him worse rather than better.

Jasmine handed me one of the canteens, and I poured the fresh cool water over his knee. He hissed as I wiped away the blood from the wound.

"You need stitches."

He nodded. "Anyone got a needle and thread on them?" Sarcasm dripped from his voice, knowing full well none of us did.

"I could cauterize it." The idea came to me out of nowhere, but I knew it was a good one. He gaped at me in horror, though he quickly seemed to understand. "It would stop the bleeding and maybe burn away any infection." I squeezed his shoulder. "Not going to lie though, it'll hurt like a mofo."

Licking his lips, he swallowed. "Do it."

"Are you sure?"

"Hell no, but there isn't any other option. Especially since we don't know if we're going to get back or not."

Taking a deep breath, I nodded. "Where's Dionysus's strong brew when we need it?"

Ren chuckled. "If only."

I poured more water on his knee, wiping it to clear away any dirt—it needed to be as clean as possible. Once I handed the canteen back to Jasmine, she gave me a curt nod in support.

Sitting back on my haunches, I took another settling breath, then squeezed my hands tightly until flames ignited over them. I focused on the fire to make sure it wasn't huge. the point wasn't to burn down a house, I just needed enough heat to sear Ren's skin together and purify the cut. I didn't want to damage any healthy skin or cells.

Once Lucian handed Ren a stick to bite down on, he sat beside him and held onto his shoulders. It was as much for support as it was to hold him so he didn't try to bolt. Logically, Ren knew that this had to be done, but when the fire started to lick along his skin, instinct would kick in, never mind adrenaline, and he would try to get away from the pain.

"You ready?"

With a grimace, he nodded.

Calming myself and focusing on his healing, I swiftly set my fiery hands onto his knee, then pulled away.

If it wasn't for the stick in his mouth, I suspected Ren would've screamed. As it was, a garbled cry escaped from around the chunk of wood.

As I'd known would happen, he jerked away from the pain. His other leg kicked out in reflex, nearly booting me in the hip, but Lucian held onto him so he couldn't move much more. I focused on my fire, trusting Lucian to hold him in place.

Closing my eyes, I pushed the heat into his flesh once more, and swiftly removed my palms, then repeated the process one last time. In those few two seconds touches, I felt his skin knitting back together. Along with the fire, I pushed into him all the healing I could, thinking of Georgina when I did, and got a small surge of extra energy.

Finally removing my hands, I pulled my fire

back into myself and leaned away. I could sense his fever breaking while clean drops dotted Ren's forehead. Sweat soaked his shirt.

The infection in his flesh subsided, the dry heat slowly abating.

His eyes had squeezed shut during the process, but he opened them again, irises filling with relief as well as exhaustion from the extreme pain.

I'd given him momentary hell, but I'd also taken some of his agony away. I was thankful for that.

Feeling drained, I fell back onto my butt. Healing him had tired me out, though it was worth it. Both Jasmine and Mia helped me to my feet, their touch was soft and cool while they led me over to the pool's shore. Jasmine pushed me down into a soft bed of green grass, and handed me a canteen. Coming over to our side, Cassandra gave me another apple, which I bit into immediately. Sticky sweet juice trickled down my chin.

"When was the last time you slept?" she asked me.

I shrugged. "I don't know. Probably longer than it is smart."

"You can't save Gina if you fall apart."

I couldn't save her if I was asleep, either, but I kept that observation to myself.

Jasmine nodded. "She's right, Mel. You need to rest. So, do we all."

"And what about Gina?" My bright best friend, currently trapped inside of a monster.

"She's tough, and smart. She'll find a way to stay safe until we can rescue her." Jasmine put an arm around her girlfriend, and they sat down on the grass nearby. When Mia's head rested on her shoulder, it looked like she might be crying. Jasmine rubbed a hand up and down her back to console her.

Maybe I should have had some pity… but I found that I did not.

The energy in the air changed when Lucian joined us, but Cassandra suddenly dropped her gaze, hugging her torso. "I'll go check on Ren," she murmured and walked away.

Her misery was palpable.

Lucian sat beside me. "What can I do?"

"Help me look for a portal behind the waterfall?"

"How about I do that, and you stay here and rest."

I shook my head instantly, trying to get up, but he pushed me down—none too gently may I add.

"Mel, you don't have to do everything yourself. I am perfectly capable. We all are, actually."

Obviously, I had hit a nerve. I nodded. "I know you are. I'm sorry."

Getting to his feet, he unfurled his wings and flew over to the waterfall. I watched as he swooped into the curtain of water, disappearing. There was a sudden flash of white light, and I suspected he was using his lightning powers to illuminate whatever was behind there.

I ached to know, impatience tightening inside of me, but I lacked the energy to keep that urgency up. Once I ate the rest of my apple, I bit into a second piece of fruit, keeping watch, but I could feel my eyelids starting to droop. Now that I was sitting in a soft spot, with all this peaceful beauty around me, my body started to shut down. In my mind, I needed it to keep going, but I'd obviously pushed myself to the limit. My battered body was ignoring what my mind wanted and taking charge.

By the time I'd finished eating and drinking from the canteen, Lucian emerged from the water-fall. He did a spiral in the air, his wings stretched—the movement not unlike a dog's, shaking after a bath to dry off. He landed softly beside me on the grassy shore, and I could still see droplets of water glistening in his hair.

"Anything?"

He shook his head, frowning. "Not that I could see. It's just a small grotto behind the falls. I dragged my hands along the stone, and there isn't anything there but rock."

"Should we tell the others?" I was disappointed, but not giving up hope yet.

Lucian looked over at Ren and Cassandra, then toward Jasmine and Mia. Everyone looked like I felt, as though we'd pushed ourselves too far. He shook his head, sending a few droplets of water flying. "Let's give everyone a couple of hours to rest." His gaze came back to me. "You too, Mel. You sleep. I'll stay awake."

"Are you sure?" I asked, even as I leaned back onto the grass. I didn't want to sleep, but even I had to admit that I needed it. We all did.

His fingers swept a stray hair from my cheek, his touch leaving warmth in its wake. "I'm sure."

Blinking up sleepily at him, I slowly shut my eyes. The last thought I had before I fell asleep was that I should tell him that I had Hades's thread in my pocket. He deserved to know that I was thinking about how to rethread it, and bring the God back to life. That I wasn't deterred from that goal, even though we had to break the spinning wheel to splint Ren's leg.

I didn't dream, not really. It just felt like I was floating in a vast sea of darkness, twinkling stars floating beside me. I was at peace, for the first time in years. Then the dark expanse started to undulate, until there were waves of ink all around me and I was swept up into them.

"Mel!"

The voice startled me, and I turned my head to find someone in the darkness.

It was Lucian.

"Mel, wake up!" His hand fell on my shoulder, shaking me.

When I blinked my eyes open. Lucian and the others were standing around me, but there gazes weren't fixed on me, they were gawking wide-eyed all around us.

"What's going on?" I rushed to my feet with Lucian's help, soon feeling the ground beneath us shudder and move. My first thought was that there was an earthquake, but the way the stone was shifting seemed too controlled for that.

"The mountain's moving," Jasmine muttered, her arm tightening around Mia.

I swung around to look behind me. The craggy rock formation was indeed moving. A thunderous creak and groan echoed around us, until the stone seemed to unfold itself. A larger pike loomed above us, moving with purpose and design.

The boulder slowly turned, and a pair of large brown eyes with moss, and tree branches for eyelashes blinked down at us.

The mountain was alive.

Heart pounding harshly against my ribcage, I stared up at the giantess. Her whole body and head was made up of stone and trees. Patches of grass and moss covered her here and there, the pattern strangely resembling some sort of toga. One arm was a solid gray mass, while the other ended with tree trunks for fingers. Those fingers were now pointed down at us accusatorily.

"Who dares to disturb me?" Her voice was like thunder, rattling everything around us, even my bones. My teeth started to ache as if I'd been clenching my jaw for hours, the vibrations echoing deep inside of me.

"Holy shit," Jasmine cursed under her breath. Her eyes were wider than I'd ever seen them.

"That's an understatement." I glanced at the others. "I'm going up to talk to her." My black wings unfurled instantly, and I flapped them once to stretch out the feathers.

Maybe this mountain giant knew something about the worm beasts, and how to help Georgina.

"I'm coming with you." Lucian's wings were already unfurled, and he lifted into the air before I could respond. Obviously, he'd already anticipated what I was going to say, and wasn't giving me that chance to say it. Namely, he wasn't letting me tell him to stay where he was, and to let me handle it.

Cautiously, we flew up to her face. I hoped she didn't swat at us with her tree hand like we were bothersome flies. That would sting.

"We're sorry to have disturbed you. My name is Melany, and this is Lucian." I gestured to him hovering beside me. "We are demigods in training, from the academy…"

"I know who you are." The force of her voice blew us back a little, her breath like a crisp wind. It took a bit more effort to remain in front of her.

"May we know who you are?" Lucian asked politely. He'd aced diplomacy. It was one of the reasons he was a leader at the academy and why Prometheus relied on him so much.

"I am Mnemosyne, the Goddess of Memory and Time." She lifted her rocky chin with pride, as if daring us to say we didn't know who she was.

I gaped at her as it all made sense. Where else would the Cave of Memory be, but inside the Goddess of Memory herself? Nearly speechless, I shook the disbelief away. This was a meeting I'd never expected to experience in my life.

"We are honored to meet you." Lucian offered, inclining his head as if he was meeting royalty. I supposed in some ways, she was. There weren't too many Gods who had been at the very start of the existence of all things. Thankfully, Lucian didn't fumble. He must have been feeling as much shock as I was, but he covered it well.

"What are you doing here?" she asked.

"We are looking for The Fates." I flew in a little closer to her face, but not too close. I didn't want to seem aggressive, yet I needed to see her clearly. I wanted to be able to recognize if she was telling us the truth.

"They are not here." The Goddess' eyes were vacant, as though she were looking at something only she could see. She probably was.

"Yes, we realized that. Do you know where they've gone? It's really important that we find them. The balance of the entire world depends on it."

"Like I said before, I know who you are, Melany Richmond. Daughter of darkness." Her eyes finally focused, narrowing as she looked at me.

I didn't like the way she spoke my name, so I flew back. Lucian must've sensed something wrong also, because he hovered to my side, placing himself slightly in front of me, as if he could protect me from the giantess.

We both knew that it was highly unlikely.

What she offered, however, was the opposite of what I expected.

"You released my Titan brothers and sisters from Tartarus." Her voice was grave, imparting the seriousness of her words. "Because of this, I will grant you one wish. It can be anything. This question you ask about The Fates, is this your wish?"

One wish. One question.

Lucian and I looked at each other. Damn it! I needed to know where The Fates went, but I also needed to know who wanted to resurrect Zeus. There was also the matter of us being stuck here, *and* Georgina being inside a giant worm. I glanced down at the ground, my gaze sweeping over the others. Even from up there, I could see the confused and wary looks on their faces. My eyes settled on Ren. He definitely needed Chiron's healer hands.

We needed so many things. I had to choose wisely.

My attention returned to Mnemosyne. "My wish is to transport all of us back to the academy."

"Mel…" Lucian sounded hesitant, but I shook my head sharply, cutting him off.

"It's the smartest choice. Together we can figure out all the other stuff."

Slowly, he nodded. I could tell he wasn't convinced, but he knew better than to argue with me.

"Very well," the Goddess conceded. "Stand together and I will send you back."

Lucian and I dropped to the ground, next to Jasmine, Mia, Cassandra and Ren.

Mnemosyne lowered her hands—one stone and one tree—until they were right over our heads. Within seconds, the air shimmered with energy all around us. As I glanced up at her, I saw that her rocky eyes glowed with power.

"I would have told you where to find Hades…" Her voice confessed in my head.

Before I could react, a portal opened beneath us and we fell through the yawning chasm.

CHAPTER FOUR

MELANY

*L*ike a big sack of rocks, we landed unceremoniously in the middle of the eastern training field. I crashed on my back and its suddenness knocked the wind out of me, forcing me to gasp for breath. The last words that Mnemosyne had said to me, whispered in my mind so no one else could hear, had left me breathless. What had she meant by telling me where Hades was? Did that mean he was still alive somewhere? In a place I could actually get to?

Hope was a terrible burden that I now carried,

along with the secret I'd tucked into the pocket of my jeans.

After a quick check to make sure Hades's thread was still there, I didn't sit on my butt and ponder it; there wasn't any time. We had to get Ren to the infirmary so Chiron could heal him and nurse him back to full health. The healing I'd been able to do for him had only been temporary, and it had certainly lacked Georgina's skill. His wound couldn't go much longer without being properly treated.

Together, we picked Ren up and flew him across the vast academy grounds to the west wing of the colossal stone estate. It was harder than it should have been, but we were all exhausted.

Inside it, we—Lucian and I, mostly—carried Ren down the wide corridor and into the infirmary. Chiron was busy patching up one of the first years, who had cut himself with a sword by the looks of the gash on his arm. He looked up, eyes narrowing when we entered.

We settled Ren on one of the cots while Chiron hurried over, the click of his hooves echoing off the infirmary walls. Intrigue entered his eyes as he took in the sight of our disheveled selves, and the pain still etched on Ren's face.

"He tore open his knee on some rocks," I offered in way of explanation, resisting the urge to apologize.

Chiron unwrapped the mess of cloth we'd tied onto Ren's leg. The scrap that Cassandra had torn from her shirt was now crusty with dried blood and other disgusting things.

"I can see that." The centaur poked and prodded the wound and the skin around it, making Ren wince with each, not so gentle, touch. "Who cauterized this?"

Prepared for his scrutiny, I lifted my chin. "I did."

He grunted and pinned me with a beady stare. "It's not bad. At least you didn't damage the healthy tissue around it."

As praises went, it wasn't outstanding, but I wasn't going to get anything better than that from the taciturn healer. He was getting as grumpy as Hephaistos over the years, and that was saying something. It probably didn't help that we were in here often, having done something dangerous, and most likely reckless. Thankfully, he always fixed us up without much preamble. He was good like that.

"What were you doing for this to happen?"

I glanced at Lucian, then at the others, unsure

of exactly what to tell him and what to keep to ourselves. "It's a long story."

"Well, you're going to have to tell someone about it, because you've been gone for over a week, and Prometheus isn't happy."

A week? I never would have guessed that. Obviously, time was getting even more messed up than before. After having spent months in the underworld with Hades, I was used to the time variances in the different realms, but it was still a bit of a shock to hear exactly how long we'd been gone.

Mia frowned, her gaze flitting from Jasmine to me, to Lucian, probably searching for reassurance. "We were gone a day at most."

I shook my head at her, willing her to hush.

Chiron shook his head too as he applied a rank-smelling poultice to Ren's injury, wrapping it up with a clean muslin cloth. Ren exhaled heavily with relief.

"You've been gone for seven days," the centaur confirmed. "You all missed your classes. The ones you were instructing had to be cancelled. Prometheus was upset, and so were the other professors who had to take on extra duties due to your absences."

I sighed. Clearly, we had some explaining to do. "Does Prometheus know we're back?"

"Yes, he does." Came a commanding voice from the doorway.

Turning, I found the seven-foot-tall leader of the academy ducking his head slightly to enter the room. He came over to where we clustered around Ren on the cot. His face was impassive, but I felt trepidation at what I knew was to come.

"How is he?" he asked Chiron.

"The wound is bad, and there is infection. Melany was able to cauterize it, which probably saved his life, but he's not out of the woods yet."

Glancing down at my friend, I realized for the first time how serious his injury had truly been. Guilt swirled inside my guts at not thinking about him and his life while also trying to figure out how to find Gina. My bestie's disappearance had seemed the more pressing of the two issues, and it was only then that I understood I might have pushed Ren too hard.

Prometheus patted Ren's shoulder, then turned his gaze, fierce when it wanted to be, on me and the others.

"I have given you a lot of leeway over the past few months, because of what you all suffered through, and because of the great debt I and the other Titans owe you. Yet, you have continually neglected your duties here at the academy, and that, I will no longer tolerate."

Lucian opened his mouth to speak, to defend me I imagined, but Prometheus cut him off instantly.

"You are reckless and careless, Melany, and I won't have you endanger anyone else."

My mouth open as well, to reply, then closed again. He was right, and I couldn't argue his point.

"Mel didn't make us go with her," Jasmine interjected, her arm still around Mia. "We chose to leave the academy with her."

"And why did you leave?" Prometheus demanded, and there was no question that we would answer him.

Jasmine glanced at me for guidance, and I knew I had a decision to make. Whether or not to trust this Titan. I'd trusted the Gods before and had been betrayed, but at this point, I didn't see any other option. We still needed information from Artemis so we could find Georgina. I couldn't let my pride get in the way of that…

If I did, I would be risking my best friend's life.

"We went to The Cave of Memory in search of The Fates," I explained, lifting my chin defiantly.

That surprised him, and his brow deeply furrowed. "The Cave of Memory? Why would you go there?"

"Because something is going on with death and time, *and* fate. I also think someone is trying to resurrect Zeus."

"For what purpose?"

That didn't sound like a shocked denial to me. Interesting. Did he suspect it as well?

"To put him back in power, I suspect. To kill me. To undo everything we fought for."

He scoffed, shrugging one shoulder. "You have an over inflated opinion of yourself and your worth, Melany, if you think someone would go through all that just to kill you. There are other things in this world to worry about."

Did I? Maybe that was true. It wouldn't be the first time someone accused me of only thinking about myself. But was everything I'd done, everything I'd dragged my friends into, the result of only thinking about myself? I didn't think so.

"Well, maybe it isn't about me. That still doesn't change the fact that someone is messing around with time and death. And someone, also doesn't want us to find out who, because when we were in the cave, two giant white worms burrowed through stone to get to us. One of them swallowed Gina just as she found Zeus's severed thread." Grief made the words taste sour in my mouth.

Prometheus's eyes widened at that. "White worms, you say? That is peculiar. They don't often stray from their lair."

"You know what they are?' Mia raised her head from Jasmine's shoulder to pipe up, but I interrupted her.

"That's why I need to talk to Artemis right away, she'll know where their lair is, and then we can go there to find Gina—"

"You will do no such thing. I will speak with Artemis and we will figure out what to do. You lot are to remain here to perform your duties to the school, and to the recruits." His voice was firm, leaving no room for argument.

"But sir," I began to protest. "I need—"

"You are to stay in the academy, Melany. If you go against this order, you will face the consequences of that action. Do you wish to put your friends in harms' way again?" He nodded to Chiron, who was still tending to our friend. "Keep me updated on Ren's condition." With those last words, he swept out of the room, moving with more grace than I thought a giant of a man could.

In his wake, he left determination, and I gathered it close.

I looked at the others. "Like hell I'm staying put." With resolute movements, I started for the exit. "I'm going to go find Artemis. She's most likely out at the archery field and stables."

Lucian caught up with me before I could leave. "Mel…"

My brows furrowed as I whirled on him. "You can't possibly agree with him?"

"Maybe he's right. Let them take care of it. They're Gods, they can find Gina a lot faster than we can." His face was unreadable and irritation flared as I looked at him.

"If it was you lost somewhere, Gina wouldn't hesitate despite the ramifications."

"That's not fair, Mel." Lucian looked like I had punched him in the gut, and truth be told, I was tempted.

"Hey, life's not fair, Lucian. Haven't you realized that by now?" I kept walking, anger swelling inside me again. Anger at being told what to do, anger at some God not believing me, yet again, when I told them about some danger coming our way. I couldn't believe that Lucian of all people, was trying to stop me from rescuing my best friend from mortal danger.

Well, he didn't get to decide what I did or did not do.

He continued to follow me as I marched down the corridor. "We can't just act before thinking. Look at what happened to Ren. He could've died."

That was a low blow, but I absorbed it and continued.

"I am thinking. I'm thinking that Gina *will die* before anyone does anything about it." I stopped walking and turned to face him. "Do you think I'm reckless and careless, like Prometheus says?" My question was almost a dare.

He swallowed before answering but kept my gaze. "I don't think you're careless, Mel. I know you care a lot about everyone you're trying to save. But you are reckless. You dive in before thinking it through. It's how you ended up in oblivion, by going off with Tisiphone that night without telling anyone, without telling me. It would've taken you five minutes to fly to my room and let me know where you were going and why."

Pausing, he shook his head.

"And I imagine Nyx told you to leave but you

didn't listen, so she sent you there. And after finding the Cave of Memory, you just bulldozed your way there without a thought of how to get home. If we hadn't literally stumbled onto Mnemosyne, we'd still be wasting away there. Ren might be dead, and Gina would *still* be lost to us."

"I may bulldoze my way into things, but you seem to follow along just fine." My tone reverberated with anger, but his words hurt.

He nodded. "I know, and that's my undoing. That is all our undoing. You are a force, Mel. It's impossible not to be drawn into your… adventures. We all know it."

My gut tightened as I searched his face. "You blame me for Gina."

Sighing, he rubbed his face. "I don't blame you."

But he did. I could see it in his eyes. He blamed me. I remembered that look from the battle, after he learned Revana had fallen into the chasm. How could he not blame me, when I blamed myself?

"Well, this is me telling you that I'm going to find Artemis, get her to tell me where the lair is, and I'm going to go there to get Gina. You don't need to follow me. I'll be fine on my own." I would have to be.

Without another word, I walked away.

"Mel!" I could hear the pleading in his voice, but I didn't stop. I couldn't. I was doing what was best for me, and for him. He probably just didn't know it yet.

I'd been walking away from him for months. It was time for Lucian to let me go.

CHAPTER FIVE

LUCIAN

I watched her walk away, angry that she was going to do whatever she wanted no matter what I said to her, even if it was the most reasonable recourse. In a way, it was what I liked about her, what had drawn me to her—her rebelliousness, her stubbornness—but it was also what was driving us apart.

She was chaos, impetuousness, and darkness, and I was starting to accept that I was the opposite of all those things. Although opposites did indeed attract—it was physics—that didn't mean those two things could or should remain together forever.

When I returned to the infirmary, Jasmine, Mia, and Cassandra were waiting there for me.

"She's off to break the rules again, isn't she?" Jasmine asked me, sighing heavily.

"Yeah." I scrubbed my face with both hands in frustration. "I tried to talk her out of it, asking her to let Prometheus do what he said he was going to do, but she wouldn't listen. She's the most stubborn person I've ever met."

"That's an understatement," Jasmine shook her head. She didn't look happy.

"What are we going to do?" Cassandra asked, which surprised me as she'd been fairly quiet during all of this. I couldn't even imagine why she'd stuck with us the entire time.

I eyed her. "You know you don't have to get involved with this anymore. I feel like you were forced into all of it."

She rubbed at her temple. "I am involved. My visions make me culpable. I don't have much of a choice."

None of us felt like we had a choice. Maybe we really didn't. After all, how could we let Mel go off on her own?

"If we follow Mel again, we will probably all be expelled from the academy. Expulsion means that our memories are wiped and we're left to fend for ourselves," I explained. I wasn't sure if she truly knew what it meant to be part of the group—to follow Melany into the fray once again.

Mia glanced at Jasmine and she licked her lips. It looked like she was having second thoughts. I didn't blame her.

Jasmine grabbed her hand. "I understand if you don't want to come, but I have to go. It's Gina. Like Mel, I can't abandon her."

"I know." Mia swallowed when her voice wavered. "But where you go, I go."

Leaning in, Jasmine pressed her lips to her girl-friend's mouth once, and then again. Their kiss was sweet and loving, and it made my heart ache.

Somewhere along the line Melany and I had lost that connection. I remembered how her eyes would light up when I was around. I hadn't seen that spark in a long time. Only when she talked about Hades... or if someone mentioned him. Even in death, he had her attention. More than I had ever had.

The loud clicking of Chiron's hooves on the tile floor signaled his approach. He handed Ren a cup of something hot and steaming that smelled Gods awful. Grimacing the whole time, Ren drank it all.

Throwing a side-glance at the healer, I assessed him, knowing full well he'd overheard everything.

"Don't look at me. I'm not going to give you a lecture about what's right or wrong. You wouldn't listen to me anyway." The healer offered us a rare half-smile.

"Are you going to give us away?" I asked.

He made a face. "I can't believe you'd ask me that after everything. You know I'm always on your side."

Once I nodded my thanks to the centaur, he left to take care of his other patient.

"Okay, so we all agree to go after Mel?" My gaze connected with each of my friends' seeing them nod all around me.

I glanced down at Ren, lying pale and in pain on the cot. As his eyes opened, he nodded as well, but I reached for his shoulder, squeezing it. "You'll have to sit this one out, bud."

"Find Gina," he murmured. "Bring her home. That'll be enough for me."

"We will."

MELANY

. . .

Marching through the academy to the outer doors, I avoided every professor and guard along the way. I'd had to slide into the shadows to escape running into Athena, and also, so I didn't bump into Heracles—although he looked like he had other things on his mind and might not have noticed me anyway.

He was muttering something about silly first years.

Once outside, I took to the air, flying over to the training field on the edge of the grounds. It sat near the stables and woods that housed the obstacle course Artemis made us go through during our first year.

In the air, I felt better. I always did when I was flying. The blast of cool air shook off the frustration and anger I'd been holding onto since arguing with Lucian.

The field near the archery targets was empty; there was obviously no class today, or it had just ended. Either way, it was good for me. It meant I didn't have to hide. I landed near the open stable doors, maybe Artemis was tending to the beasts housed and fed in the individual stalls. Before I entered though, I heard voices from the inside. Artemis was talking to her brother, Apollo—I could recognize his baritone anywhere now—and by the pitch of their voices, they were in the midst of an argument.

Shadows swirled around me like a cloak of night, responding to my silent call, and I slipped into the barn unnoticed.

"I can't believe you're getting involved with this," Artemis accused. "We've never taken sides before. Not even during the great Titan war."

"It's not right what happened. It's thrown everything out of balance. Surely, you see that."

"Zeus is gone, Hades is gone. Sounds about balanced to me. I was getting tired of their infighting."

I crept in closer, careful to muffle my footsteps, and saw Artemis brushing down one of the fire-breathing horses. Apollo stood next to her, his whole body stiff and uptight, which was his usual demeanor.

"We are Gods, Sister. And we *share* power with some unruly mortals who don't deserve—"

"They are demigods now."

Apollo spat onto the barn floor. "They are inferior."

"I never thought you to be an elitist, Brother." She gave him a leveling look. One I wouldn't have cared to be on the other end of, if I were him. "That is how the great war happened; Zeus wanted to have all the power, and not share it."

"I wanted to give you a chance to join us."

"Join with *her*, you mean?"

"Yes."

Artemis shook her head. "I will not join you, but I will not stand in your way either. You are my brother, and despite of all your failings—especially in this—I still love you."

Who was *her*? Was it Hera?

Why must there always be a plot afoot?

Apollo tipped his head, then stormed out of the barn. Thankfully, he did it through the opposite doors, and didn't need to pass by me. When he was gone, Artemis put away the brush on the wall of the giant horse's stall.

"You can come out now, Melany. I can hear you breathing." Her voice was cool and neutral.

Damn it. I should have known that I couldn't hide from a Goddess. I swallowed, afraid she was going to do something, but I stepped out of my cloak of shadows, and approached her regardless—

my chin lifted. She was a fierce fighter, skilled in bow, dagger, and sword alike, but so was I.

"Who is Apollo joining? Is it Hera?" I asked, my words defiant after deciding to just come out swinging. "Is she trying to resurrect Zeus to kill me?"

Artemis' expression gave nothing away as she regarded me. "I'm not sure what you think you heard, but you really do have an overactive imagination." Walking out of the stall, she locked it up behind her. "Prometheus told me you'd probably come here, doing the one thing he told you not to do."

Of course he had. I decided to let the conversation I overheard go for now. Georgina needed me, and I wasn't going to argue with someone who I knew wouldn't tell me shit.

"I want to know where the white worms' lair is. I need to rescue Gina. She's in danger."

The Goddess nodded. She wasn't surprised. "Prometheus has already informed me of the situation."

"Okay, great. Then, let's go." My large wings unfurled, flapping behind me. The motion disturbed the big fire horse, and he stamped his huge hooves onto the ground, snorting through his nostrils. Curls of black smoke floated away.

Artemis led me out of the barn. "Georgina won't be in any danger. White worms don't eat people."

"She *is* in danger. Someone commanded the worms to attack us and take her." I spoke insistently. "One of them swallowed her whole."

This did seem to surprise Artemis, but she blinked the reaction away. "I will tell you what I told Prometheus. I will go to their lair and check on the situation. If Georgina is there, and in any type of danger, I will rescue her and bring her back to the academy."

"I'll come with you."

"There's no need, Melany. I am perfectly capable of handling this, and you have responsibilities here." Artemis seemed completely unruffled.

"Fuck my responsibilities! Gina's in trouble and I need to find her. I don't know why no one is helping me, why you don't see this as an emergency." I frowned at her, an idea dawning. "Unless you know something I don't?"

Her eyes narrowed and she took a step toward me. "You need to calm down."

There was little in the world that I hated as much as someone telling me that.

"Calm down? Why would I calm down when

my best friend could be dead? Killed by some big, fucking worm that someone sent to stop me from finding the Fates." Tiny flames ignited on the tips of my fingers. I could feel the rest of my powers swirling around in my gut, ready and willing to be unleashed, though I still had enough self-control to understand that unleashing them on Artemis would be a very bad idea.

"Your paranoia, isn't helping anyone, Melany."

"I'm not paranoid."

Was Artemis gaslighting me? Was that what was going on? Because something didn't make sense here. They were trying to convince me that there wasn't someone trying to resurrect Zeus, that someone wasn't out to get me?

"You're acting irrationally. Maybe you should take some time to think in your room at the academy. Get something to eat and get some sleep. You look exhausted."

"Like hell." I unfurled my wings and was about to lift into the air, when Artemis grabbed me by one wing and tugged me backward. It wasn't a gentle tug; a few of my feathers fell in her hand when I pulled away from her.

I was startled. Stupidly, I'd thought that Artemis would be on my side—our side. That she would help. I guess I shouldn't have been surprised. She was a Goddess, after all.

"Melany, don't make this difficult. All anyone wants to do is to make sure you're thinking straight, and that you're not a danger to yourself or others."

Shit. I was the one in danger here. They were trying to stop me from finding out who wanted to resurrect Zeus, and why they were playing around with time and death.

"Why are you doing this to me, Artemis? I've never thought of you as an enemy."

Her face softened as she took another step closer to me, her one hand reaching for me. "No one is doing anything to you, Melany."

Her words were meant to be calming, but all I could focus on was her other hand that fluttered at her side, closest to the dagger strapped onto her belt. I had a sense that she wouldn't hesitate to use it on me if I forced her.

Glancing around, I considered my options, my every sense heightened. I could dissolve into the shadows, but she was standing too close. Artemis was within grabbing distance for sure. I could move fast, but maybe not fast enough. She was a Goddess of battle and knew how to subdue an enemy quickly.

Before I could make a decision, three other people swooped down from the sky. Two of them were academy guards, outfitted in armor and carrying swords. I'd dealt with them before, on more than one occasion.

The other was Hera.

I was most definitely in trouble.

"Hello, Melany." Her voice was sickly sweet, reminding me so much of Aphrodite, though I didn't think she'd appreciate the comparison.

Instead of looking at her, I gauged my chances of getting out of there. I was up against two Goddess, but I wasn't without resources. My eager fingers wriggled at my sides, preparing to create some lightning so I could blast the two guards. Yet, after that, I wasn't sure I'd be quick enough to portal through the darkness before either Hera or Artemis were on me.

Artemis would likely use her blade, and I knew she was quick. I'd seen her in battle. She had the power to turn people into animals or plants. Although, I hadn't seen her use her powers, I'd heard about what she could do, and had done in the past. There were a few plants around the grounds that were rumored to be past lovers of Zeus's.

I wasn't sure if I believed it or not, but I didn't really want to take the chance to find out. I had no intention of being turned into a tree.

"What do you want?" I finally asked her.

"To bring you back to the academy. Everyone's worried about you." She smiled, the curve of her lips saccharine sweet.

I laughed without humor. Others might have fallen prey to her charms, but I knew better. "Oh, I doubt that."

"You're acting irrationally," she added with that pasted on smile of hers. "I mean, you used my portal, in my hall, without my permission. You have to realize that your actions have consequences."

"And what about your actions?"

Her brow furrowed. "I beg your pardon?"

"I know you sent the white worms to the cave to stop us."

"I'm sure I don't know what you're talking about, Melany. You're making no sense whatsoever."

Aside from hearing her words, I also caught the conniving glint in her eye. It told me everything I needed to know.

I didn't have the time or resources to be afraid. I rubbed my hand against my pocket, thinking about

Hades to give me strength and courage to do what I needed to do. The golden thread in my pocket seemed to tingle with energy, giving me a burst of strength.

Before I could overthink it, my hand shot out, sending a bolt of lightning that hit one of the guards in the chest and knocked him to the ground. His chest armor instantly scorched. With my other hand I pulled the shadows to me, wrapping them around myself like a cloak.

I wasn't quick enough.

Before I could suck in my next breath, Artemis had an arm around me, and her dagger pressed to my throat right underneath my chin.

Hera patted my arm with a patronizing lift to her lips. "Don't fight. It's pointless. Just come with us back to the academy, and everything will be right as rain. I promise."

Right as rain for them, maybe. Not for me.

"Wait until Prometheus hears about this," I sneered with as much bravado I could muster. An image of the giant, seven-foot God flashed through my mind's eye.

Hera clucked her tongue, and a frothy laugh spilled from her lips. "Silly girl, who do you think sent me?"

CHAPTER SIX

LUCIAN

*A*s we burst out of the main academy doors, I stopped midstride, my heart thudding hard against my ribs, and pulled the others to the side behind a clumping of blooming lilac bushes.

"What's wrong?" Jasmine asked.

Silent, I gestured toward the cobblestone pathway leading up to the academy, where a group of people walked with an easy stride. In the lead, wearing her royal blue robe, was Hera. A guard in full golden regalia walked behind her, and following that guard marched Melany—her hands fisted at her sides, lips pressed together in a tight line.

To a stranger, her expression might not have revealed much, but I knew her. She was pissed. Right on Melany's heels was Artemis, dressed in battle gear, and it looked like she had her dagger in her hand, ready to use it at any moment. At the rear was another guard, the only difference was that his armor wasn't shiny and gold. It was scorched as if someone had thrown fire or lightning at him.

My money was on Melany being that someone.

I felt a swell of pride. Good for her.

What was going on? Why did they have her under guard? What did she do? As far as I knew, she'd only gone to talk to Artemis about finding the lair of the white worms. Obviously, something else must've happened.

I thought of Ren, injured from the adventure in the Cave of Memory. Of Georgina, in the belly of one of the worms. I might not have agreed with Melany's stubbornness or insistence on doing things herself, but I did agree that we didn't have time for this right now. Not if we wanted to get Georgina back, preferably alive.

"It looks like they're arresting her, or something," Mia murmured from beside me.

"I know. I don't like it. It doesn't feel right."

"Do you think Hera is trying to stop Mel from rescuing Gina?" Jasmine asked.

"She's trying to stop her from something that's for sure." My fingers itched at my side, ready to create some lightning.

"What are we going to do?" I could see that Jasmine was also itching to act. Tiny flames had already started to form on the tips of her fingers.

"We're going to create a distraction and get Mel the hell out of there, before they can lock her up in a cell and we won't have any way of getting to her." I turned to Jasmine. "I'm going to create a lightning storm. A big crazy dangerous storm. I'm not sure how long I can control it, but once it's up, I need you and Mia to swoop in and grab Mel."

I just hoped it would work.

"I can help you," Cassandra piped up from behind us.

My gaze swung to her, surprised. Not that I didn't appreciate the help. "Do you have lightning skill?"

She shook her head. "No, but I have some control over light. I discovered it during Demeter's earth powers class. She said not many people have that power."

I wasn't sure how light could help us, but maybe

she could generate enough of it to blind Hera and the others. It certainly couldn't hurt.

"Okay, that could be useful. Cassandra and I will come around to the front of the academy, while you two fly up toward the back. When the storm happens, that's your cue to fly in and get Mel. We will only have once chance to do this."

"Once we have her, what do you want us to do?"

"Get the hell out of here."

Jasmine's brow furrowed, looking from me to Cassandra. "What about you?"

"Don't worry about us. We'll be gone before they even know what hit them."

Although I said the words, I wasn't sure I believed them. So many things could go wrong, but we had to do something. I couldn't let Melany be imprisoned for whatever reason trumped up by them. She needed to find the white worms and get Georgina.

After a brief nod to them, Jasmine and Mia dashed away from the cobblestone path, keeping low to the ground so as not to be seen, and disappeared behind some trees. I looked at Cassandra. "Are you ready for this?"

"No, but let's do it anyway."

"I'm going to form some lightning in the sky. Can you brighten it?"

She nodded, determined. "I think so. I will try."

Looking up at the blue sky, I concentrated on pulling together all the ions in the air. It didn't take long for sparks to ignite along the clouds and draw attention. Hera's head came up, and I saw her face pinch with concern. Not enough to stop the march to the academy though. Not enough for her to go into defensive mode either.

She was a Goddess, after all. As far as she was concerned, what could we possibly do to her?

Relentless, I kept gathering the ions faster and faster, until the first bolt of lightning flashed across the sky, producing a loud crack of thunder in its wake. The sound was enough to shake the bushes where Cassandra and I were hiding. The smell of ozone grew, thick and heavy in the air.

That got Hera and Artemis's attention. Hera waved her hand in the air and the procession stopped, her keen eyes scanning her surroundings. Artemis shouted something to the guards, and they moved to box Melany between them.

Another bolt cracked across the air, then another, until it was a cacophony of thunder and bright blinding flashes of light. Unfortunately, it still wasn't enough to draw their attention away from Melany. We needed something else, something bigger.

Glancing back at Cassandra, I wondered how she could help. She was crouched on the ground, with her eyes clamped shut, and her hands curled into fists. I was about to reach out and touch her to get her attention, when her skin started to glow with a yellow hue. Like a light bulb had been switched on inside her body. I watched as it grew brighter and brighter until I had to shield my eyes.

Suddenly, a bright globe appeared in the sky, it was as bright as the sun, growing to the size of a massive boulder. It was actually quite frightening to witness. If I didn't know what I was looking at, I would've thought someone had detonated a nuclear bomb.

The rays pierced the sky, harsh and unrelenting, black spots forming in my vision from looking at it too long. She'd conjured up a temporary sun, it seemed, but I didn't have time to marvel at it.

Hera and the others brought their hands up to shield their eyes from the glare. Yet, the light was so intense it seemed to press down on them somehow. The two guards beside Melany turned their heads, and one even put up his metal shield to protect himself. He sunk to his knees as the light pushed down on him.

It was just the thing we needed.

Out of the corner of my eye, I saw movement atop the trees. My head turned in time to see Jasmine and Mia swoop down like eagles fishing in a lake, heading toward the group on the cobblestone path. Melany must've known it was us doing our best to get her the hell out of there, because she immediately unfurled her wings and shot up to join her rescuers.

Jasmine managed to grab onto her arm while Mia hovered in front of them, thrashing out with her legs, so the guards couldn't snatch Melany from the air.

Without hesitation, Artemis swung her bow off her back and nocked an arrow, but Melany had already formed a dark cloud around the three of them, hiding them. The Goddess fired anyway, yet it didn't hit anything—at least I assumed it didn't. Melany, Jasmine and Mia had already vanished inside the shadows.

Now Cassandra and I needed to get away before we were discovered.

Reaching for Cassandra I touched her shoulder and felt a surge of heat flare up my arm. It wasn't entirely unpleasant, more like that moment when you realized you had spent too much time in the sun, but before it began to hurt. Her eyes snapped open to look at me, irises as golden as the sun she'd created out of nothing.

"We need to go."

Nodding, she relaxed her body, and the big, glowing ball in the sky blinked out of existence. The air seemed cool in its absence.

I grabbed her hand and pulled her up, sprinting together out of the bushes and toward the maze. It was easy to get lost in it, and I'd been through it so many times, I knew its secrets and the perfect places to hide. Over the past two years, our group had even created new alcoves and concealed spots, ones that the Gods didn't know about yet.

Commotion and shouting came from behind us. The sound of boots thumping on the ground echoed around us.

"There! Shoot them!" It was Hera yelling commands.

An arrow thunked into the stone statue guarding the entrance to the maze—mere inches from my face. I knew it wasn't a mistake. Artemis didn't miss. It was a warning shot, and I'd likely only get one.

"Stop! Or the next arrow will go through her neck."

The *her* Artemis was referring to was Cassandra. The Goddess knew one of my weaknesses. Protecting others at the detriment to myself. It was a lesson that she and others had tried to push out of me, but they always failed because I would never consider that a weakness. Something to overcome.

It was part of who I was, at the heart of my authentic nature. I was proud of my loyalty to my friends. In my opinion, it was a strength to nurture not to destroy.

I stopped running, yanking Cassandra to halt at my side and pushing her a little behind me. We turned to face our attackers.

Hera's eyes narrowed as she regarded me. "Where has she gone?"

I shrugged. "I don't know who you are referring to."

"Your loyalty to Melany will be your undoing, Lucian." Artemis shouldered her bow and quiver of arrows.

"Yeah, I don't see it that way." I lifted my chin in defiance.

A humorless chuckle escaped Hera. I wasn't even sure the Goddess knew what humor was. In the years at the academy, I'd only seen her smile once or twice, and it always seemed to be when one of us was in trouble. She had a sadistic streak. No wonder she was a match for Zeus.

"You will learn to see it that way soon enough, dear boy." She stepped in closer to Cassandra and slowly looked her up and down, like she was choosing a piece of meat to devour. She sniffed down the length of her regal nose. "I don't even know who you are."

"She's a first year. Her name is Cassandra," Artemis offered with a smirk. "She's a favorite of my brother's. A strong prophetess."

"Well, it won't help her now." Hera clucked her tongue, a moue of false sympathy on her lips. "You, girl, will learn the folly of your choice of friends."

Cassandra's head lifted in defiance as she stared at Hera, surprising me.

I thought she might cower at the weight of the Goddess's fierce and judgemental gaze. A grin blossomed across my lips at her bravado, I couldn't stop it. Everyone had been so quick to assume the prophetess was weak, including myself, because she didn't seem to have any power beside her visions— and now her light ability.

However, Cassandra had a steely resolve and fortitude that I'd not seen in many people. I liked it.

The guards, stoic and unemotional, marched to our sides to lead us away from the maze and toward the academy. I sighed, happy that we'd been able to do what we'd set out to do. Rescue Melany. At least now she was free to follow Artemis to find Georgina.

"Now that this is under control," Artemis unfurled the huge expanse of her golden wings. "I can do the task Prometheus has given me without interference." She rose into the air, and flew back toward the stables.

Out of the corner of my eye, I saw movement in the shadows and I smiled to myself, not wanting to give anything away to the enemy. Knowing that Melany would do whatever she needed to find Gina and bring her home gave me relief.

Whatever Cassandra and I faced inside the academy would be well worth it.

CHAPTER SEVEN

MELANY

"Thank you for getting me." I hugged Jasmine once we were safely on the ground, encased in the shadows a good fifty feet away from Hera and the others. It was difficult to stay cloaked while flying so we had to land. "I thought I was done for."

"Of course we got you. We got each other's backs, no matter what." She nodded at me matter-of-factly.

I was so happy and relieved to hear her say that. Since I'd managed to escape from oblivion, I'd been feeling out of sorts. Out of place. Somehow, I had a sense that my friends were feeling that way too. Being wiped out of existence sure had a way of messing up things. It toyed with the mind, and I knew we were all feeling the effects of it.

Although, my friends probably didn't understand why they were feeling it, because they didn't possess those memories of their lives without me anymore. It was just a ripple of uncertainty, skimming across the skin like a shiver of dread.

"Where's Lucian?" I asked.

"He's with Cassandra. They were the ones who made the distraction. Although, I have no idea who made that sun appear out of thin air."

Yeah, I had questioned that as well when I saw it grow in the sky like a ball of shimmering liquid gold. I didn't think Lucian had power like that, so that left Cassandra. She was full of surprises, that one. I liked that about her. As unpredictable as a storm.

We had that in common, I thought.

"Where are they?" I hoped they hadn't been caught.

"Just outside the main doors, near the huge lilac bushes."

When I grabbed Jasmine's hand, she grabbed

Mia's too, realizing I was going to be taking us through the shadow portal.

"Hold on." I took us deeper into the darkness as I pictured the spot she mentioned, wrapping us in shadows. Seconds later, I could see the front doors of the academy through the inky haze of the dark curtain thrown over us. I didn't see Lucian or Cassandra, and my stomach fell.

"They're not there."

"Maybe they're hiding somewhere else," Jasmine offered.

"Or maybe they got caught." Fear tinged Mia's voice.

My gut clenched as I shared her thoughts. Would Hera take out her anger and frustrations of losing me on them? She wasn't a patient of kind woman, so I didn't like the possible answer to that.

Urgently, I looked around the area, trying to guess where Lucian would go. Where would be the safest place for them to hide? My gaze landed on the maze in the distance. There were plenty of places to hide out in there and Lucian knew most of them. We'd spent a lot of time in the maze during our first year here, trying to discover all its secrets. Creating our own.

Using the shadow-ways, I moved us closer to the

maze just in time to see Lucian nearly get skewed with one of Artemis's arrows. Luckily, he didn't, but I knew it was only because she purposely missed. He'd be dead otherwise. There was no one better with a bow and arrow than the warrior Goddess.

"Where has she gone?" Hera's words reached us where we huddled, cloaked in the darkness.

Obviously, she was asking about me.

Lucian shrugged with that smug laziness he could project from time to time. I remembered it clearly from when we first met. "I don't know who you are referring to."

"Your loyalty to Melany will be your undoing, Lucian," Artemis warned, slinging her bow and quiver of arrows onto her back again.

"Yeah, I don't see it that way." He held her gaze in defiance, and my chest tightened at the sight. I loved that he defended me even now. Even after all that we'd been through, after all I'd put him through.

I hoped I never lost the faith he put in me, that I would always deserve that allegiance.

"You will learn to see it that way soon enough, dear boy." Hera stepped closer to Cassandra, looking down her nose at the red head. "I don't even know who you are."

"She's a first year. Her name's Cassandra," Artemis offered. "She's a favorite of my brother's. A strong prophetess."

"Well, it won't help her now." Hera clucked her tongue. "You, girl, will learn the folly of your choice of friends."

The guards moved in, taking up posts beside Lucian and Cassandra, but his gaze flickered over to the deep shadows along the bushes—right where we were hiding.

Lucian was looking for me.

It took everything I had not to burst out of the shroud, take up arms, and free him along with Cassandra. But I couldn't. He'd risked it all to rescue me, I couldn't foolishly throw that away. We wouldn't get another chance to find Georgina.

There was a big ole red target on my forehead, so I would've definitely been in danger if I'd gone with Hera into the academy, but I didn't think there was that same level of risk for Lucian. He was well liked. Well respected by both recruits and many of the professors, even if Hera or Artemis were the ones to level his punishment, it wouldn't be grave.

His demise wouldn't go unnoticed or unchallenged. Mine might have. I'd gained a lot of enemies in the past couple of years, so there was probably a sign-up sheet for a chance to take me out and betray me. Hera's name was obviously first on that list, and I wondered who else I would see on that page.

I looked at Artemis and wondered if she was an enemy. She wasn't an ally, not in this. She might have been during the war with Zeus, but with this—whatever it was—she firmly stood with her brother, Apollo, who was definitely on the evil side. I couldn't trust her, but I didn't have to, to get what I wanted.

And what I wanted was to find Gina and bring her home.

For a moment, I thought Artemis was going to go with Hera and the guards, but then she unfurled her wings and took to the sky.

"Let's go," I whispered to Jasmine and Mia.

"Can we follow her in flight while cloaked?"

Glancing to the horizon in the direction she took, I suddenly knew where she was headed. Back to the stables.

"I'm pretty sure I know where she's going."

"Okay, let's do it." Jasmine nodded.

With one last look toward Lucian, I gathered the shadows tighter, wrapping us in them like a snug blanket and transported us back to the stables.

We beat Artemis there, settling a good distance from the structure, and watched as she flew in and landed just outside the doors. She'd sensed me earlier, so I wasn't going to make the same mistake by creeping in closer. I didn't need to be, I knew what she was doing.

A few minutes later, she burst out of the stables riding an eagle-faced griffin. The beast let out a squawk then soared into the sky.

"Shit. We're going to need to fly to follow her." Jasmine shook her head. "We'll be out in the open. She'll see us for sure."

I walked to the barn doors and peered inside. "Not necessarily." Leading Jasmine and Mia to the stalls, we stopped where the huge, black, fire-breathing horses lived. "These guys can run as fast and as far as the griffin can fly."

The lead horse, Aethon, the one that had belonged to Ares, stomped his hooves and snorted when he saw me. Black curls of smoke came out of his nostrils. I'd ridden him before, during the obstacle course trial to the surprise of everyone—especially Artemis—and he seemed to recognize me.

Both Jasmine and Mia looked like they were going to wet their pants while staring up at the large beasts. "Are you sure they'll let us ride them?" Jasmine swallowed when one of the horses approached her, its red eyes aflame in its sockets.

"I'll ask." My hand reached out toward Aethon. "Hey, remember me?" He snorted again, but sauntered over toward me, until his nose pressed up against the palm of my hand. I smiled. "Who's the fiercest beast of them all? You're better than any old griffin, aren't you?"

Aethon whinnied and stomped his front hooves. The sound echoed through the stall.

"I'm going to take that as a yes." With a chuckle, I opened the stall door and went inside. Grabbing onto his long black mane, I pulled myself up onto his broad and sturdy back. "Hurry. Mount the horses. We can't lose sight of Artemis."

Jasmine helped Mia onto one of the other stallions, jumping onto the back of the last one. They were a little smaller than Aethon, so they didn't have that much trouble. Once we were all set, we sped out of the barn, single file. I noticed that Artemis had flown west, so I steered Aethon that way, going through the wooded alcove that had been the obstacle course. Soon, we were galloping at a quick speed, so much so, that I had to hang onto his mane not to fall.

As I glanced over my shoulder, I found that Jasmine and Mia did the same thing.

When we burst out of the trees and into a meadow, I spotted Artemis in the sky—about one hundred yards in front of us. I patted Aethon on the side. "I knew you wouldn't let a griffin best you."

With adrenaline shooting through my veins, we rode across the land that encompassed the academy grounds, through more woods, and then up to the lake. Artemis flew over the water while we had to go around it. I knew it would cost us precious time, but it couldn't be helped. As Aethon and the other horses galloped along the shoreline, I kept my eye on the Goddess and the direction she was flying.

Once we crested the corner, I lost sight of her as I came up onto the other side of the lagoon, but as soon as we cleared another gathering of tall trees, I spotted her again. She'd brought the griffin down closer to the ground—near some cliffs, and a waterfall. Artemis steered the beast toward the tall, roaring, curtain of water.

It was another portal. It had to be, because I was certain that the white worms didn't live in this world.

"She's going through a portal!" I pointed out at

the same time that Artemis flew the griffin through the cascade. "We need to hurry, so we don't lose her!"

I patted Aethon on the flank to encourage him to follow, and at first, I wasn't sure he was going to do it. He seemed a bit skittish as we neared the thunderous sound of the waterfall.

"You can do it! You're the mighty Aethon," I patted him again. "I know you're not scared of anything."

Small flames shot out of his nostrils when he snorted loudly, galloping into the pond. The water rose up to just under his belly, with no sign of slowing, but it didn't stop him. We all crashed into the waterfall the next moment, crossing it. I half expected to just end up running into a stone wall, but there was a shimmer there, and I could see another stretch of land beyond it.

Holding my breath, I pressed my heels into Aethon's side, and urged him forward, unsure of exactly where we were going to end up on the other side.

It didn't matter. As I thought of Georgina, I knew that we had to go.

CHAPTER EIGHT

MELANY

*T*hrough the portal, Aethon galloped out onto solidly packed dirt plains with a triumphant snort. I patted his side. "Good job."

Glancing over my shoulder to make sure Jasmine and Mia were still with me, I found them both wide-eyed and shocked that we had made it. Jasmine gave me a thumbs up and I reciprocated. Mia looked pale but she continued forward, and we headed across the plains, sand dunes, and mud flats in the distance, looking for any sign of Artemis.

We rode along the bank of a river that snaked through a shallow gorge. It wasn't long before I spotted the golden-winged Goddess in the sky on the horizon. It appeared she was slowly descending on the back of the Griffin.

"She's there," I called back, pointing her out to the others.

Keeping our eyes on the precise location that Artemis descended, we rode faster. The river took a wide curve then we came up onto a straight stretch of mud flats, with a few small dirt and sandy hills alongside. That had to be the place as I saw the Griffin ascending back into the sky but Artemis wasn't on its back

I wondered if she knew she'd been followed. Gods help us if she did.

"Spread out and look for a hole in the ground, or a tunnel in one of the dunes." I steered Aethon over to a small hill that was made mostly of gray dirt. There were probably some rocks in there too, but it was no mountain, that was for sure.

"Here! I found a large hole!" Mia called out after a few minutes.

Jasmine and I joined her at the gaping hole in the mud. It definitely looked big enough for one of those white worms to move through it. It wasn't as big as the hole I'd run through in the cave, but still wide enough.We all dismounted and considered how we were going to get down there.

Crouching along the edge, I created a small ball of fire, and dropped it inside it. It hit the surface within six feet, its light spreading as though the tunnel took a turn. I had a feeling this was going to be more like sliding down a complicated waterslide, than just dropping into a wide chasm like we did when going to Tartarus.

I stood. "Okay, seems like we're going to be climbing down, and shimmying through a tunnel."

Mia shuddered. "I don't know if I can do it."

"It's okay." Jasmine's hand ran over her shoulder reassuringly.

"Yeah. No one's going to force you to go down there. Can you stay here and take care of the horses?" She nodded "We're going to need them to get out of here after we get Gina."

"But I feel bad for not—"

"Don't." I shook my head. "This," I waved my hand to gesture to us as a group, "We're not the Gods' army. We're more than that. And I'm definitely not the general."

Lucian might have disagreed with that proclamation, but he wasn't here.

"Okay. Thanks." I could hear the relief in her voice but also the guilt.

Running a loving hand through her hair, Jasmine hugged her.

"Can you help lower us down?" I asked before I got on my knees, and swung my feet over the edge of the hole.

"Of course." Mia lay on her stomach at the edge, gripped my hands, and helped me until my feet touched the dense soil.

I reached the first twist in the tunnel without a problem. Now, it was a matter of hunching over a little to walk through the next section.

As I faced it, I was acutely aware of the fact that this time there was no rope around my waist, held by my friends, who were ready to pull me back at the first sign of peril.

Jasmine dropped down behind me, while I started through the next leg of the tunnel. There was no light down here, the blackness absolute, so I formed another ball of fire, tossed it front of me and then kicked it forward. . So, basically, it would be a kick the ball, shuffle-shuffle-shuffle, kick the ball again kind of situation.

After the third kick, the orange orb disappeared. I realized where it went when I came to another drop in the passage. Extending my arms, I braced myself against the walls, so I didn't fall blindly and I could peer into the lower shaft.

The flames flickered not that far below me—maybe seven or eight feet. The air smelled musty, and thanks to the dim illumination, I saw the fine particles of dust and grit that surrounded me, dancing through the air.

"We're going to have to grip onto the edge again and drop down. It's not too far."

"This sucks," Jasmine moaned.

"I know."

I swung around so my feet hung over the empty space to slowly lower myself, holding onto the edge. Grabbing my hands, Jasmine helped me the rest of the way. When it was her turn, I reached for her legs and held her until she could let go and land safely.

We did this maneuver another three times, until we came to a tunnel that opened up into a hollow dug out of the dirt and mud. There was some sort of light source ahead, so I snuffed out my fire ball. Plus, I didn't want to announce our arrival.

It was cool down there and a shiver rushed over my body as I slowly inched my way to the opening and peered out. The light source happened to be a couple of torches stuck in sconces along the grotto walls. Worms didn't need light, so they were lit for someone.

Artemis maybe? Someone else?

My suspicion grew when I heard voices coming from somewhere in the cave. I couldn't make out the words, but it was definitely two female voices. Unfortunately, because of the echoey acoustics, I couldn't quite recognize either one. I assumed one of them belonged to Artemis... the other? Hera, possibly. Yet, if that was the case, then she'd used a different portal to get here, and would've had to use it shortly after I saw her marching Lucian and Cassandra into the academy.

It was almost impossible it was her. Then who was it? Who else would want Zeus resurrected?

"Do you see Gina?" Jasmine whispered into my ear as she pressed up against me along the tunnel wall.

Squinting in the low light, I couldn't see much of the hollow, so I had to lean out of the opening to get a better view. Slowly, I made my way, crab walking on the hard-packed mud floor so I could see more of the area. After a few steps, a vacant expanse of flooring extended before me, and in the middle of it lay Gina. She was folded into a ball, hugging her knees while her eyes were closed. She was still alive. For now.

Fear tasted bitter on my tongue.

My head turned toward Jasmine and I nodded. Relief lit up her face, and the breath she had been holding in anticipation escaped her. Using my hands, I told her that I was going to move closer to Gina, and she was to stay there to keep a look out for us.

After receiving a thumbs up from her, I did a sweep of the vicinity before moving any closer. It seemed like the coast was clear, since I couldn't see the Goddess or the worms. Taking in a deep breath, I made a dash for Gina. Before I could reach her though, I spotted Artemis coming out of a small alcove, she was adamantly talking to someone who I couldn't quite distinguish. They remained shrouded in the shadows along the cave walls. I dived behind a mud bulge coming up from the ground.

"I won't be part of this," Artemis declared. "It's the same thing I told Apollo."

"It's too late for that," the other person argued. Her voice seemed deep, but it could've been the hollowness of the cave messing with the timber and pitch. I felt like I should've recognized it. Like a bad dream that faded upon waking.

"This girl is innocent. You need to let her go."

"No one is innocent. She had Zeus's thread on her, I sensed the power of it. Besides, I expect a certain amount of collateral damage. Such is the case in war.

Georgina wasn't collateral damage. She was a person. She was my friend. My best friend. I wasn't going to sit here and let anything happen to her. Resolute, I decided to go grab Georgina. Even if I expose myself, I had enough powers to defend us both, I was sure of it.

My attention traveled to Jasmine, who was now ducked behind another dirt formation. Our gazes met and I pointed to Georgina, indicating that I was going for it. She shook her head and waved at me to come to where she was.

I couldn't do that. It was now or never.

Taking a strengthening breath, I dashed out of my hiding spot toward Georgina. Swiftly, I crouched at her side and tapped her face to wake her. Relief washed over me like a cool wave when she moaned, and her eyes blinked open.

She was alive! Thank the Gods. I'd never been so happy.

"Mel?" Her voice cracked.

I grabbed her arm to help her up, but she had a

hard time standing, so I had to pull her to her feet. "We need to get the hell out of here before—"

An ear-piercing shriek cut off my sentence. *Shit.* I guess we were spotted.

"Kill them!"

My gaze met Artemis's as she swung around toward us, an arrow already nocked in her bow, but she didn't let it loose. She could have quite easily, and I had no doubt in my mind that it would've imbedded somewhere in my body.

Why had she hesitated? Regardless of her reason, it was the second we needed to get in motion.

An arm around Georgina, we ran to where Jasmine waited. Just before we reached her though, the very air around us seemed to vibrate, knocking us off balance. Bits of dirt and tiny pebbles fell onto our heads from above us.

Another shriek pierced the air, and I turned to see Artemis had loosed her arrow, but not at us. Whoever had been obscured in the darkness was struck by her weapon, and was not happy about it.

Interesting. Was Artemis on our side after all?

Jumping to my feet, I yanked Georgina up with me, and continued to run to the tunnel. When we reached Jasmine, she took Georgina from me and helped her into the opening. Before I went through it, my gaze searched for Artemis again.

The Goddess writhed on the ground, her face knotted in severe pain. Some kind of electrical charge wrapped around her like a giant boa constrictor, but it wasn't the white thread of lightning, it was dark purple, the color of a throbbing bruise.

As her head snapped back from the pain, our gazes met.

"Run!" she screamed, and unsheathed the dagger at her belt. Artemis scrambled up to her feet and sprinted into the dark grotto, wailing with a war cry. It spoke greatly of her power that she could move at all with that unholy thread wrapped around her.

I didn't wait to see the outcome of her attack, just dove into the opening right behind Georgina and Jasmine. The way back seemed longer, but that was probably because death was hot on our heels, and Gina was in rough shape. We had to help her up at each turn along the shaft, but by the time we reached the final passageway up, we had it down to a science. Mia was there on the last one to help pull her out of it.

Jasmine's girlfriend drew on a reserve of strength I hadn't anticipated she had.

Once we were all topside, I looked back down into the hole. "I need to go back and help Artemis."

"No." Jasmine grabbed my arm, her fingers digging in as she tried to catch my full attention. "She's a Goddess, she doesn't need our help. Besides, it looked to me that she wasn't innocent in this scheme."

"That may be, but she helped us get away. She fought with us against Zeus when she didn't have to. I can't let her die down there." I knelt down at the edge of the hole, intending to drop back inside, but a ground shaking screech came from below us.

Oh, no.

I scrambled away just in time to see a white worm shoot out of the hole. Another worm exploded out of the mud nearby, and then they both slithered across the mud flats, desperately retreating from something. Before any of us could do anything other than run to the horses, the ground shook beneath our feet, and the hole caved in. With a loud thump, one hundred yards of dirt, mud, and rock collapsed in on itself, creating a giant chasm.

Everything that had been in those tunnels and

the cave was buried under a thousand tonnes of earth. There was no way anything, or anyone, could dig themselves out of there.

Shocked to my core, I gaped at the giant sinkhole that spread out before us. My heart thudded hard against my ribs, picturing Artemis buried beneath all of that. Georgina came to my side and curled a hand around my arm. Part of it was to hold herself up, but the other was because I could see how horrified she was feeling, same as I did.

"Maybe she survived," Jasmine offered from my other side. Her voice was quiet, unsure.

I didn't respond because I didn't hold out any hope of that. We both knew better. The Gods were strong, seemingly invincible, but not completely immortal. They could die. We all knew that. We'd all seen it.

There was nothing we could do for Artemis. It had to be enough that we'd saved Georgina.

"Are you okay?" My arm wrapped around Gina.

She nodded. "I'll live." Her voice was filled with bravado, but I alone heard the underlying tremor. Whatever she'd gone through would haunt her. She'd have to learn to live with it, the way we all learned to carry on despite our battle scars.

"What happened?"

"It's a bit foggy, but after I was swallowed, which was not fun by the way—being inside a big worm is gross—I remember being spit out into the cave, and then not much else until you arrived."

"You didn't see anyone before we showed up? Artemis was arguing with someone. And I'm not certain it was Hera."

She shook her head. "Nothing concrete. Just shadows."

Relief coursed through me once more, and I hugged her, so incredibly happy to see her again in one piece. "I'm glad you're okay. Nothing we can do about Zeus's thread now."

"I know." She shrugged. "How's Ren? Were you able to get him to Chiron?"

"Yeah, he's okay. Chiron's taking care of him."

"Good. He was on my mind the entire time I was down there."

"Okay." I turned to find Aethon so we could mount up and go home. "Let's get out of here, then you can see Ren for yourself."

CHAPTER NINE

LUCIAN

*S*weat dripped down my face and back as I put the last of the metal scraps into the large wooden bin, rolling it over the forge to throw them into the fire and be melted all over again. The effort and standing so close to the fire made me sweat even more. The contained metal had to be around one hundred and fifty pounds, give or take. My arms and shoulders were screaming from exhaustion, and my whole body was going to ache tomorrow from the work.

I understood now why Hephaistos was so strong.

This was part of our punishment for interfering with Hera's plan to detain Melany. We had to clean Hephaistos's forge from top to bottom. I'd been tasked with doing all the heavy lifting while Cassandra was on the bottom level, mopping up the stone floor with the most volatile smelling solution I'd ever encountered.

Hephaistos assured us it wasn't toxic, but I didn't know how when it burned my nostrils even from up here. I couldn't even imagine how Cassandra was dealing with it. After we finished there, we had to go to the kitchens and scrub the floors, counters, and ovens.

Manual labor was hard, tiring, but it beat the alternative. It definitely could have been worse if Hera had had her way. Maybe torture? Prison? Neither of those prospects would have surprised me. I'd seen Zeus do as much. Sometimes I still had nightmares about the torture Melany endured at his hands, and the agonizing pain he'd forced Apollo to inflict on me. Every now and then I got a headache that felt like an ice pick to my brain.

I had gladly accepted it, because if she was preoccupied with us then she wasn't going after Melany.

Thankfully, Prometheus had intervened as

Hera and the guards marched us down the back corridor of the academy—toward the dungeons. He was the one who had determined our punishment, and I suspected he'd gone easy on us. It also made me think that he was more on our side than we assumed after the chewing out he'd given Melany.

Once I emptied the ponderous bin of metal, I walked down the precarious stone steps to the bottom floor, to see how Cassandra was doing. Following the stench of vinegar and bleach, and who knew what else, I found her finishing mopping up near the shelves in his storeroom. The place where he kept all the shadowboxes he had made over the past year. They were still all there on the shelves and I wasn't sure if this was for the new batch of recruits or if these were the ones still left because there hadn't been a list of recruits to send them to for their eighteenth birthday, although Prometheus had told Melany that had been a clerical error. It was obvious the Fates' disappearance had far-reaching ramifications.

I wondered briefly just how profound those ramifications would be.

Startled when I suddenly came up beside her, Cassandra nearly knocked over the bucket of dirty, bleachy water. A hand clutched her chest, and she stared at me with wide eyes.

"Sorry. I didn't mean to scare you." I tried to smile, but I was so exhausted that I suspected it came out more like a grimace.

She was likely too tired to notice or care.

Cassandra shook her head. "You'd think by now I would have run out of things to be scared of."

Her and me both.

"Yeah, I think I stopped jumping at every strange thing I saw after the first six months here. Although Medusa still kind of frightens me whenever I see her." That snake hair of hers was just creepy.

"Me too. I'm also deathly afraid of the Furies. I don't know how Melany handles them."

I chuckled. "Me either. Sometimes I think Mel actually likes them." The humorous mood dimmed as I thought about her, and all the danger she'd been involved in with them. Even going as far as trusting them. Mel had followed Tisiphone without a second thought.

"Sorry," Cassandra murmured, jostling me out of my thoughts. Her tone was cautious. "I didn't mean to bring up something painful."

"It's fine. It's not painful. Pisses me off actually.

I was just thinking about how Mel just left without telling anyone. Without telling me. And ended up in that place." I shook my head. "I mean, if she hadn't found a way back home… I'd be, I mean, I wouldn't have even known. It's impossible to think about to be honest."

Cassandra's attention went back onto her mopping. "Yeah, it's weird to think about."

I watched her, studying her face. She'd been different after we fished Melany out of the lake. She'd been the one to get us there to rescue Mel after seeing a vision about a blue-haired girl, just as I had supposedly dreamt about her. Yet, I didn't remember those dreams. I didn't remember anything really, not before Melany was in my arms —all wet and shivering. Only that she'd gone missing, but something I overheard Melany saying to Cassandra in private had me thinking that maybe it wasn't the same for her.

"You remember, don't you?"

Cassandra's head snapped up and she frowned. "What?"

"You remember the time when Mel was gone. You kept your memories when we all lost ours."

Avoiding my eyes, she continued to mop the floor. It told me everything I needed to know.

"We should finish up in here so we can get the work in the kitchen done. I also think I need a break. My hands are starting to hurt from holding this mop for so long. I probably have splinters."

My hand reached for hers, stooping her.. "You know, that is the most I've ever heard you say since I've known you."

She stared at my hand over hers, as if I'd somehow hurt her. Hurt her or… something. "Can we just do our work and be done with it?"

"Tell me."

Finally, her gaze met mine, and there was something in her eyes that made my heart ache. "You don't want to know, Lucian. Trust me. It'll be too hard to understand."

"Tell me. I can handle it." I dropped my hand.

"Well, maybe I won't be able to." Putting the mop in the bucket, she slid it to the corner. "I'm going to the kitchen now. Hopefully, there will be some lunch left." Cassandra attempted to walk away, but I moved in front of her.

"Cass, please tell me. I have to know."

"Don't call me Cass." She bit down on her lower lip. "That's what you called me in that reality, and it hurts to hear you say it."

"It does?" My brow furrowed, confused. "Why?"

"Because we were together!" she snapped. "We were a couple, Lucian. And we were happy."

What?

I flinched back, completely blindsided by what she'd just uncovered. I hadn't expected that at all.

Cassandra tried to go around me again, but I grasped her arm to stop her. Her skin was hot beneath my palm. "You can't say that then walk away."

"Why not? What's the point of talking about it? You love Melany. You guys are together. Knowing there was a time that she didn't exist, and you were so very happy with a girl like me is not going to change that."

Tears gathered in her eyes, a silver sheen illuminating them, and it made my gut twist into a knot.

"I'm sorry. I wish that I could remember." Something tickled at the back of my mind. Not a memory, more like the promise of one, but it was gone before I could even take a breath.

She shook her head, her smile slightly bitter. "No, you don't. I wouldn't wish this for anyone. It totally sucks."

My hand dropped from her arm, releasing her,

and I shoved it into my pants' pocket. What a mess. "Lately, I'm questioning whether we are even together anymore."

I wasn't sure why I said that, why I was even telling her. I supposed I'd wanted to talk to someone about it, but there hadn't been anyone. It also seemed like the right time. We'd been in a state of danger and chaos for so long now, that I kind of didn't know any other state of being.

She sighed, and I thought for sure she was going to leave. "You can talk to me about it if you want."

"It feels different between us."

Melany no longer look at me the way she once had. She tried to hide it, but I could tell. That was how well I knew her.

Cassandra glanced at me knowingly. "Yeah, of course it does. You've both been through a lot. I assume you've changed since first coming here."

"Yeah, that's true." I just about ran a hand through my hair, but stopped, realizing my hands were dirty with grease and soot from throwing metal into the forge. "Mel isn't the same girl who I found splashing around in the ocean at the wrong pier."

"And you're not the same guy either. How could you be after all you've suffered."

"I don't know what to do. She's pushing me away…"

"And you're trying to hold onto her with both hands."

"It's that obvious?"

She gave me a "Yeah, duh!" look.

"What do I do? Let her go? I don't even know how to do that."

"You know the saying, 'If you love something, set it free…'? There's some truth to that." A bittersweet smile curved her lips. "Trust me. I know."

"But what if she doesn't come back?" The thought of it made my stomach clench.

"Then it wasn't meant to be, and you would need to move on." Her hand gently patted my shoulder. "You won't die without her, Lucian. I know that firsthand."

Gazing into her eyes, I saw truth and honesty there. I tried, reaching deep into my mind, to remember her in the other reality. It felt like there was definitely something there… if I focused hard enough.

I caught a glimpse of a scene. It was just a flash, and my mind struggled to hold onto it, to make sense of it and give it form and sound. It wouldn't take a solid shape, nothing concrete that I could trust. It was far from being a memory.

However, if I closed my eyes, I could see her smile. When I did that, there was no mistaking the warm feeling that blossomed inside of my body. Like honey, thick and sweet, it slowly flowed through my veins.

Exploring the feeling, I reached over, and interlaced my fingers with hers. "I may not really remember anything, but I feel like you and me, as a couple, would makes sense. I can picture it."

Cassandra lifted her head fully, and a smile flourished across her face. It was *the smile* that tried to form in my consciousness. The one I was sure she'd given me on many occasions. The smile I admittedly didn't deserve.

Unexpectedly enjoying the warmth of her fingers entwined with my own, I tugged on her hand. "C'mon, let's get out of here and head to the kitchen. Wwe can find some lunch. I'm starving."

"Me too."

We left the forge and made our way up the stone staircase to the main floor. "I bet you like ham and cheese sandwiches with a dollop of honey mustard."

Laughter escaped her. "I do like that. It's my favorite sandwich."

I nodded. "Not a bad guess."

She gave me a look, then turned away. "Nope, not bad at all."

And I was sure it was a guess. It didn't feel like a memory. Not really, but right now, I wasn't certain about anything. My world was getting turned upside down. Again. Which was just another typical day at the Demigods Academy.

CHAPTER TEN

MELANY

*T*he trip back to the academy was quick. Georgina didn't appear to be injured, and she insisted on not needing to be looked at, but I was determined to get her to the infirmary so that Chiron could check her out anyway. Since she wanted to see Ren, she could just let the healer do his job while we were there. Gina didn't argue after that.

When we arrived back at the stables, we put the horses into their stalls and made sure they had food and water. I spent a little more time with Aethon, brushing him down while I figured out how to explain Artemis's death. I was having a hard time reconciling it in my mind as well.

Silently, I wondered who was going to look after all the animals now. Maybe one of the recruits who had been relegated to her hall. Rosie, maybe.

After we finished with the horses, we flew back to the school. Nerves churned inside me when thinking about entering, because I wasn't sure Hera wouldn't be waiting for me with the intention of detaining me anyway. And now, with Artemis's death, I didn't know what was going to happen. Maybe it wasn't the best idea for me to even go near the academy.

I had that thought a bit too late.

The moment we stepped through the main doors, and into the looming foyer that had been so imposing and spectacular since the first day, we were ambushed by Hera and her guards. Prometheus, and a raging Apollo were there too, and it seemed like they had all been waiting for us to arrive.

Apollo was the first to act. He rushed me, eyes wild with fury. "You killed her!"

It didn't take much to figure out who the *her* was in this equation. What I wanted to know was how did he know?

I backed away from his grasping hand, setting my right leg back to get into a defensive position. It was instinctual now after years of training. My lightning power rushed to the surface, swirling there, just waiting for me to release it.

Georgina immediately stepped in beside me. "Mel didn't kill anyone. The white worms cave collapsed, and Artemis couldn't get out in time."

"You're lying!" Apollo growled, "I had a vision. I saw her wrapped in shadows and darkness, suffocating. Only Melany possesses that power since Hades' death."

Obviously, that wasn't true, because I hadn't killed Artemis. Someone else owned that kind of ability. Hera didn't, so it definitely wasn't her down in the worm's lair. Who was it? I couldn't even begin to guess. I needed time to figure it out.

"Someone else was in the cave, but I don't know who."

Hera sniffed. "Of course she's going to say that to defend herself."

"It's true," Jasmine argued.

"Did you see this person?" Hera asked, with one eyebrow cocked.

Jasmine swallowed. "I didn't, but we could hear her voice."

Apollo wasn't having it. He wanted revenge on me, I could see it in the way his eyes glowed white hot with violence and rage.

He lunged at me once more, and his hand wrapped around my throat before I could defend myself. My air was instantly cut off... I couldn't breathe. Over his shoulder, I saw Hera's lips twitch upwards into a sly smile.

Jasmine, Mia, and Georgina all shouted out to advocate for me.

It was Prometheus who put an end to it.

"Stop." His voice boomed throughout the foyer, sounding very much like Zeus. "Let her go, Apollo."

At first, the golden God ignored the order. His hold didn't loosen, instead it tightened. Frantically, I tried to pry his fingers away from my neck, but he was too strong for me, so I did the only thing I could. Fire and lightning erupted from my digits, zipping around his hand and up his arm. The sound of his skin sizzling reached my ears, but he didn't relent. A smell of burning flesh filled my nostrils, and my stomach roiled over in revulsion.

Abruptly, Apollo's seared hand dropped—blackened from my power—and he backed away.

Stumbling backward, I set my hand onto my

throbbing throat and gulped in air. I was surprised he hadn't crushed my windpipe. Any more pressure and he would have. I could barely swallow.

"She must be punished," Apollo spat. "I won't let my sister's death go without being avenged."

Prometheus lifted a hand to stop his argument. "If she is guilty, she will be punished, but this is not how we go about it. There will be a fair trial."

Trial? Holy shit! Was I under arrest or something?

I tried to speak, but my throat hurt too much to let out more than a squeak.

"She's been at the center of a lot of deaths at the academy," Apollo pressed. "Obviously, we all know she killed Zeus…"

"She was defending herself," Georgina countered. "And the rest of us."

"And there was the unfortunate death of another recruit," Hera added.

She was talking about Revana, and I wanted to cross the foyer floor to plunge my dagger into her heart, for bringing it up and using it against me.

"Aphrodite and Ares have both fallen under her hands, I'm told," Hera continued.

"For all we know, she killed Hades and took his power for herself. With him gone, she could rule the

CHAPTER 10 123

underworld herself. Maybe this has all been a power play." Apollo glared at me, until his hatred burrowed into my very soul.

Speechless, I just stared at him. I couldn't believe he thought that about me. That anyone would think that. Surely, he didn't truly think me so Machiavellian.

Slowly, my eyes roamed the other faces in the room, and what I saw nearly drove me to my knees. It was clear there were others at the academy who shared the same thoughts. I looked at my friends. Did they also think I had that kind of trickery and deviousness inside me? That I was capable of some-thing so heartless and insidious?

Both Jasmine and Georgina reached out a hand toward me. At first, I didn't know why, but when my knees touched the stone floor I realized they were trying to catch me as I collapsed.

"Take her to the dungeon," Prometheus finally pronounced. "We'll set up a day for a trial."

Two guards in shiny golden armor pushed Jasmine and Georgina aside to grab my arms and haul me to my feet. More showed up swiftly, until there was at least eight armed men surrounding me, like I was some dangerous criminal.

"You can't do this!" Jasmine shouted. "It's not right."

"They're lying!" Georgina insisted.

Mia had yet to say anything. She looked like a deer caught in headlights and I almost felt sorry for her. All of this probably seemed like way too much to handle. Even I was having a hard time dealing with it. It was all so surreal.

Me, being carted off to jail for murder. The way Apollo spun it, it sounded like I was a mass murderer, out for blood and power. In a way, he made me seem just like one of them. If the stories I'd read in the picture books as a child were true, then I'd finally achieved Goddess status.

Absentmindedly, I thought if Hades were here, he'd probably chuckle at the absurdity of it all. Then, he'd blast every single one of them and whisk me away through the shadows, back to his bed in the underworld.

As I was taken down the corridor, I rubbed my fingers over my pocket where I'd stashed his severed life thread. In my mind, I spoke to him.

'What do I do?'

For the first time, in a long time, I was scared. The last time I could remember being actually frightened was when I first met the Furies—Hades had forced me to train with them. I'd been so weak then, I thought. So much had happened since.

I wasn't the same person. I was stronger, smarter, fiercer. I possessed more power than I ever thought possible... but I wasn't a murderer, was I?

'What do I do?'

'Wait it out. You'll know what to do when the time comes.'

Hades's voice came through as clear as a bell, and I smiled.

CHAPTER ELEVEN

MELANY

Footsteps echoed on the walls while I paced the small detainment cell like a wild animal. They'd fixed up the place since the last time I was down here, breaking out Lucian and the others. I supposed they had to, since our battle with the guards had destroyed the floor and the cages themselves. I wondered if they'd reinforced the wall that led to Hephaistos's forge. That had been the way I used to break in here. Maybe I could use it to break myself out, if I could get out of the chamber itself.

I tested the bars again, and like before they were enchanted, spelled, or something to stop me from using my powers on them. They wouldn't melt with my fire, or change the configuration of their metallic elements with my earth powers. Water wouldn't do anything for me either, except maybe flood the place, but I'd drown. Any lightning would likely just electrocute me. I'd also tried to pull the shadows to me, but something was blocking me from doing that as well. Basically, I was fucked.

Tired of pacing I sat on the narrow stone bench along one wall. If I was going to get out of here, I needed a rational head. Lucian would laugh at that. He called me irrational a time or two in the past couple of years. He was probably right. I had acted impulsively in the past. It was probably what had gotten me to this point.

Frustrated, I scrubbed my hands over my face. I couldn't believe I was in this situation. Waiting to be tried for murder. It was way more frightening than having faced Zeus's torturous lightning trial. Scarier than fighting a chimera, or battling the typhon. At least in those situations I knew I could physically fight my way out of them. I believed in my abilities for battle. I didn't fear death.

Yet, I did fear being locked up for the rest of my life. I was scared of being banished from the academy, and having my memories stripped from my mind. It had been the same sort of agony I faced while in oblivion. I was ever thankful that Hecate had stopped me from drinking from the river.

Resting my back against the wall, I brought my knees up and wrapped my arms around them, pressing them to my chest. For the first time in a long while, I felt like crying. How did it come to this? Was I really that misunderstood? Was what I've been doing all this time so wrong? Had I taken an immoral path? Had I turned into the very thing I thought I'd been fighting against?

Surely, Prometheus and the others could see that everything I'd done was for the academy, my friends, the people of Pecunia and beyond. I'd never wanted power. I didn't come to this place seeking it.

But it had come to me, hadn't it?

I'd been the first recruit in history to pass all twelve trials. I had developed all the elemental powers, able to use them all at once, and beaten Zeus when no one else could. I tamed every dark beast and captured Hades's heart. Charon had even told me that the underworld was mine if I wanted it.

The truth was, I'd be lying to myself if I said I didn't want it. If I didn't want to be its ruler.

Stretching my leg, I wriggled my fingers into my pants' pocket and pulled out Hades's golden lifeline. Slowly, I rubbed my fingers on it over and over, enjoying the feel of the silk on my skin, imagining it was his skin I was touching.

A hand lifted to my face, dragging the smooth thread over my cheek, then under my nose, wishing I could still smell him. He carried the scent of darkness and danger on his skin, and it had been like a drug to me. I constantly craved it, would do anything to possess it. My eyes fell closed and I inhaled deeply…

His scent filled my nose.

Suddenly, I was back in his hall. In the wide, black stone corridor with high vaulted ceilings that led to the several rooms. Rooms I knew well. I looked down to see I wore a low-cut, black velvet dress that dragged on the floor. I didn't wear any shoes. The coolness of the black stone caressed the soles of my feet as I took a step forward.

Firelight emanated from the narrow slits in the

juncture of the wall and floor, casting an eerie glow across the smooth surface and guiding my way to the last door on the right.

My gaze traveled across the room when I entered, to the floor to ceiling shelves holding meticulously organized books by the thousands. I'd raided that bookshelf a few times during my stay in the underworld. Several Renaissance paintings on the wall witnessed my approach, including the one of Persephone, as I walked to the massive dark stone fireplace. A fire crackled inside, and I could feel the heat of it fanning my cheeks.

I sat in one of the high-backed decorative chairs, and picked up the delicate wineglass that sat on the round mahogany table—filled with what I knew would be a surprisingly sweet red wine. The first sip confirmed I was right, the taste of it tickled my tongue, and glanced over at the other chair.

Hades was there, sipping wine from another glass goblet. He was dressed in his signature dark purple suit, shiny black hair slicked back from his hard, angular, and handsome face.

"So, how does it feel to be hated and feared?" He studied me over the rim of his glass.

Not really wanting to say, I shrugged, because I was afraid of the answer.

"You can be honest with me, Melany. You know I won't judge you. Judgment is for uptight losers." He chuckled under his breath, and the rumble of it sent a shiver over my skin.

"I'm not hated or feared," I finally mumbled.

"Sure you are. That's why you're in the dungeons."

"It's just a misunderstanding."

His eyes narrowed. "Is it though? I think Apollo and Hera are both determined to have your head on a platter. They're drama queens if you ask me." Finishing his wine, he set the glass down with an audible clink on the table.

"I didn't kill Artemis."

"I know you didn't, darling. But it doesn't matter what I think. I'm dead."

I jumped to my feet and stood in front of him. "I don't want you to be dead."

Hades looked up at me, his gaze so penetrating that it made me shiver. "I know."

"I can bring you back. I have your thread. I just need to find the Fates so they can weave it back together."

"I appreciate your tenacity, Melany. It's admirable how far you're willing to go for me." He stood, his body only a few inches from mine, and I ached for him. "But is it truly the right thing to do? You should let me go and move on with your life."

"I don't want to. I want you back in my life."

He licked his lips. "I want you too, Melany. Always and forever."

My fingers itched as I stared at him. I couldn't stand there and not touch him. It was too torturous. I sprung forward and wrapped my arms around his neck, pulling him closer. With another low chuckle, his hands immediately slipped into my hair, and he tilted my head back, bringing his mouth down on mine.

His kiss was like fireworks. Every nerve ending in my body exploded with pleasure.

Gods, how I missed that feeling of total and complete surrender. He could destroy me with just his lips—and had done so, right there and then.

The next moment, he walked me backwards to press me against the wall. Just like that first time. When I lost my body, my heart, and my soul to him. If he was trying to convince me of giving up my attempt to resurrect him, he was doing a piss poor job of it. How could I give up on him when his lips were on mine, his tongue dipping inside my mouth? And his hands... his hands were everywhere, possessing every inch of my body.

I couldn't get out of my dress fast enough. Then I was naked, so was he, and our bodies pressed against each other with fervor. My hands streaked across his chest and back, reveling in the silky soft skin stretched over the hard planes of his muscles.

Instinctively, I knew this was only a dream. I knew I was in a prison cell, curled up on an uncomfortable stone bench and passed out from exhaustion, but Gods damn, it felt so real. Like I was truly with him in the library of his hall.

"Hurry." I panted into his hair while his mouth explored my chin, my throat, the spot just below my ear that he knew drove me wild. "Hurry, before I wake."

Hades's head rose and his eyes bore into mine a moment before he claimed my lips again, sweetly this time, and all sense of reason drained out of me. He'd possessed me. There was no denying it. There was no escaping it.

"It could be like this always," he murmured, resting his forehead against mine.

"How?"

He didn't respond and I became desperate. I shook him, and his head came up, his eyes were just black holes in his face.

"How?!"

Then I was alone, my back resting against the wall, and I felt so cold, my body wouldn't stop shaking.

"Hades!" I screamed until my throat ached.

My eyes snapped open as I jerked awake. I was back in the cell, huddled on the bench with my knees pressed to my chest. Using the sleeve of my shirt, I wiped at my face. My cheeks were damp with tears. I hadn't cried in months.

The dream had been so real, I could still smell the burnt wood from the fireplace, still taste the wine on my tongue and feel Hades in my hands. I rubbed my fingertips together, trying to exorcise the sensation away. It wouldn't help me with the fight I had coming.

Standing, I stretched out my legs and back. I'd cramped up from being in one position for so long on the hard, unforgiving stone. I went to the bars of the cell, and pressed my face against them, trying to catch a glimpse of someone.

"Let me out of here! This is bullshit!"

My throat still hurt from Apollo's effort to choke me to death. I needed water, food, and rest, because there was no fucking way I was going to stand for this quietly. If they were expecting a repentant child, cowering under the pressure of authority, they were greatly mistaken. Honestly, they should've known by now that I wasn't some little girl frightened by Gods and monsters.

I had become both.

CHAPTER TWELVE

LUCIAN

"I want to see her." Defiantly, I stood in front of Prometheus in his office, head high, determined not to leave until he allowed me to visit Melany. The giant looked back at me in a way that would have made most people quake.

When I'd heard that Melany had been arrested for Artemis's murder, I was stunned. Cassandra and I had just finished cleaning the kitchen, and were enjoying the fruits of our labor by gorging on beef stew and freshly baked biscuits—care of Dionysus, who just happened to be a culinary whiz, which had been a huge surprise. We heard the excited whispers of gossip spreading through the dining hall during dinner. Felt the curious looks in our direction. Diego had burst through the doors and told me about what happened.

I immediately flew through the corridors, quite literally—to the chagrin of the many people my wings smacked along the way—to track down Jasmine and Georgina and find out everything that had happened. I found them in the infirmary with Ren, whose condition had not improved. He was still pale and shaky. Chiron was doing a quick assessment of Georgina when I arrived, then he left us to talk.

"What the hell is going on?"

Jasmine looked weary, exhausted, and there were tears in her eyes. "We were ambushed when we walked into the academy. There was nothing we could do. It would've been impossible to fight our way out of it."

"What about Artemis?"

"She was down there in the worm's lair, arguing with someone else—"

"Who?"

She shrugged. "We don't know. None of us saw anyone. Melany said she heard another voice…"

"We were attacked as we left," Georgina continued. "We thought Artemis was going to kill us, but she told us to run. When we got topside, the cave started to fall apart, and the whole thing collapsed. Even the worms got away. There's no way anyone survived that, Goddess or not."

"And she was arrested for murdering her?" I was missing something here, or maybe we all were. Where was the evidence?

"Apollo was there, he was enraged. He said he had a vision about Artemis's death, and totally blamed Mel for it. He went on about Zeus's, Hades's, and even Revana's death. Apollo accused her of murdering them too, and demanded she should suffer the consequences."

I shook my head. I couldn't believe this was happening. It didn't make any sense. "What did Prometheus say?"

"Not much of anything." Jasmine scowled, her hands bunching into fists. "He's a coward if you ask me. She's responsible for his release from Tartarus. He should be thanking her not locking her up."

After a quick check on Ren, I immediately flew up to Prometheus's office which previously belonged to Zeus. Strangely, there were no guards posted at the entrance, which was customary when the God of all Gods lived there.

Prometheus stood in the middle of the room, as if he'd been waiting for my arrival.

I offered no small talk before making my demand.

"You can't see her," he answered, his tone brooking no argument. "No one can see her until the trial."

"How could you even let this happen? She saved you, don't you remember?" I paced the room in front of him, anger fueling every step. This wasn't fair.

"I do remember, Lucian, but that doesn't negate the seriousness of the accusations rallied against her."

"Ridiculous allegations. Mel would never intentionally hurt anyone, let alone kill them. She has always acted out of self-defense, or in defense of her friends and everyone in this academy. Zeus was going to kill thousands, if not more, in pursuit of power. Hades sacrificed himself for her, and Revana… that was a casualty of war. Mel tried to save her but couldn't."

"And Artemis's death?"

"I don't know, I wasn't there. But I believe my friends when they tell me it was a tragic accident." I scowled at the God. "They could have been hurt as well. They could have been killed. Why would they put themselves in danger like that?"

"And were you there when Revana fell?" His voice was patient, cool against the heat of my anger.

I stopped pacing and glared at him. "No, but I believe——"

"And Hades? Did you see his death?"

"No." My teeth and jaw clenched so hard that they started to ache. Why was he questioning everything? "Are you insinuating that Mel had a hand in all of these deaths?"

Sighing, Prometheus went to sit down in one of the high-backed leather chairs near the floor to ceiling windows that encircled the entire office. He turned his gaze to the world outside the glass, and for a long moment, he seemed to be lost in thought.

"No. But I've seen what absolute power can do to a God, let alone a mortal. She possesses more power than it is normal. I can see it swirling around her every minute of every day. Her aura is black with it."

I couldn't believe what I was hearing. Yes, Melany had a lot of power, but she'd only ever used it for good. "Nope, I refuse to believe that about her. You don't know her like I do. You only see what you want to see. There is more to her than her powers. She has a huge heart, bigger than she probably even realizes. And she loves her friends. Her loyalty is fierce."

"Lucian, I don't doubt the fierceness of her loyalty, I just question who she is loyal to. From what I've heard, Hades's death nearly destroyed her. They say she's changed. Is this information true?"

It wasn't not true, but not necessarily in the way he meant. "Death changes everyone. Or it should, if you're a decent human being."

He sighed again, nodding. "Your devotion *to her* is admirable. I can see how much you care about Melany. But do not let love blind you to the possibility that she's acting on her own best interests. That she's doing the only thing that makes sense to her right now, out of grief and anger."

I hated that he gave voice to something that had been swirling around deep inside my head. Something that I didn't dare consider. Maybe she'd been warning me about it the whole time by pushing me away.

"If you won't let me see her, how can I help her?" I felt helpless. It wasn't a feeling that sat well with me. Every fiber of my body longed to run, scream, push, fly—whatever it took to help Melany.

"The trial will be in a couple of days. Apollo, Hera, and others who have grievances against her will have an opportunity to speak. She needs people there to speak to her true character. Witnesses to her triumphs, and to the deaths that she's been accused of causing. Rally people for her defense. She is going to need it."

A couple of days? That was so soon. Good thing that she had so many loyal friends to jump to her aid.

"Why are you doing this?" I asked. "I know you can't possible believe these accusations."

"Because I am not a dictator. Unlike Zeus, I don't wish to force my will on others. I want to run this academy with a bit more diplomacy, and with that comes compromise. I can't wave away Apollo's claims. There has to be some due process. There have to be consequences to actions. Aphrodite and Ares were punished for their part in Zeus's plans, just as Zeus was punished for his actions."

"You can't compare what they did to what Melany has done." This was ridiculous. What Melany had done was nowhere near the severity of the crimes of the Gods he listed. Not even close.

"And why not? Because you're in love with her?" He waved his hand toward the exit, sighing heavily as he did. "Go and do what you can before the trial. The truth will come out one way or another."

Accepting his words even thought I really didn't like them, I nodded. Before I left though, I asked the one question I was afraid to utter, because I wasn't sure I could handle the answer. "What happens if she's found guilty?"

Just saying the words out loud had my stomach doing a slow roll of dread.

"I'll have no choice but to lock her away in Tartarus for the rest of her days." His voice was firm, and I knew that I'd get no further help from him.

Prometheus would do what he saw as fair, even if in the end, it actually wasn't.

When I left his office, I went right back to the infirmary, to see if Jasmine and Georgina were still there. They weren't, but Cassandra was sitting next to Ren's bed. In my haste to find out what was going on with Melany I'd left her in the kitchen.

"I'm sorry for leaving you without a word," I offered, immediately upon seeing her.

"It's okay. I understand. Jasmine filled me in on what happened. It's a bit unbelievable." She shook her head, as though she couldn't understand what was going on. I knew how she felt.

"It's bullshit. It's just another way for Hera and the others to stop Mel from exposing them."

"Is there anything we can do?" Her brow furrowed with worry.

I nodded. "Yeah, we need to rally the troops. Get everyone, recruit, God, whoever we can to come to her defense. The trial is in a couple of days, so we haven't got much time."

"I'll do what I can."

"Thanks, Cass. You're a good person. A good friend."

Her lips curved into a small smile. I felt the whisper of an urge to stay, to comfort her, but she gestured toward the door, pressing me to go.

I left her instructions to track down Jasmine, Georgina, and Mia to get them talking to people. We all needed to do outreach to find those who would support Melany. I decided to start with the professors, a more difficult task since they were colleagues of Artemis, Apollo, and Hera.

My first stop was at Hephaistos's forge. It had taken everything we had in the past to get him to fight with us in the war against Zeus, but I was hoping he'd be easier to convince of rallying around Melany.

Maybe the fact that Cassandra and I took such care when cleaning his forge would count in our favor. I could only hope.

"You better not be here to knock down my wall to break Melany out of the dungeons." Was the first thing he muttered to me when I found him in the forge. Not a hello or how are you, just that. "Took months to fix it after she used it to break *you* out of them."

I'd been hoping he wasn't going to bring that up.

"Nope, not going to break her out." I shook my head, offering what I hoped was a winning smile. "I'm here to ask that you speak for her at her trial. They want to prosecute her for murder. It's Gods damn ridiculous."

"Whose murder?" His words were gruff, void of emotion. It was typical of him, and honestly, at that moment, I was just thankful for the lack of drama.

"Artemis, Hades, Revana, and even Zeus's. Anything to keep her down."

"And who's they?"

"Hera and those who side with her." I swallowed past a lump in my throat at the reminder of just who Melany was up against.

Sliding the piece of metal he was forging into the cooling bucket of water, Hephaistos shook his head. Steam rose from the water as it hissed, creating a moist cloud in front of the God. "I thought all of this shit would be over with Zeus gone. It's getting old, this bickering."

"They want to resurrect him. That's why the Fates have gone missing, and Death is taking a holiday. It's all connected."

He tore at his heavy canvas clothes, and scrubbed the stubble on his misshaped chin. "I've been dealing with a few millennia of drama and betrayal, it's tedious and boring."

"Is that a yes, you'll speak up for her?" Did I dare to hope?

He gave me a sharp nod of his head, then went back to his forging. I would have preferred to hear him say it out loud, but I was afraid that if I pushed him, he would retract his agreement. So, I nodded in return, then left before he could change his mind.

After securing Hephaistos, I talked to Heracles, who was definitely going to be there for Melany, then popped in on Demeter and Dionysus. The two of them were out back in one of Demeter's many gardens, sitting on the grounds smoking weed. No surprise there.

"I take it you've heard what's going on?" I asked them.

"Yup, sounds pretty messed up." Dionysus took a hit on the joint then passed it to Demeter. Once his hands were free, he reached for the opaque water glass sitting on the table in front of him. I would have bet my wings that it held anything but water.

"It is messed up. Can I count on you two to be there in Melany's defense?"

Dionysus shrugged. "I don't know, man. We don't normally like to get involved."

What they normally liked to do was exactly this —drink wine and get high, floating blissfully through their days. It seemed I was going to have to push.

"You got involved when we were fighting against Zeus." I reminded them.

"Yeah, but Hera is way scarier than Zeus ever was. Besides, she's got Apollo, Hermes, and Poseidon on her side." Dionysus sounded like he just didn't want to exert that much energy. It would ruin his vibe, man.

"Athena hasn't decided yet," Demeter added

casually.

"That's true, and I'm pretty sure Poseidon's only involved because he's sleeping with Hera."

Anger surged through me. "We're not picking sides for a game of dodge ball for fuck's sake. This is Melany's life. She could end up in Tartarus forever. Have you ever been to that place?"

Dionysus shook his head.

"It's not a nice place to spend any amount of time in. So, pick a damn side!"

Dionysus's eyebrows lifted. "Okay, man. Chill. Of course we'll be there for Melany. Right, Dem?"

Demeter looked at me, then nodded. "Yeah. You can count on us."

"Thank you."

I left before I rescinded my thanks, and told them exactly what I thought of them and their indecision.

Next, I flew to the Hall of Knowledge to find Athena. I needed to convince her to side with Melany. She wasn't there, and I couldn't find her in any other place I thought to look. So, I checked with a few other instructors at the academy, including Erebus, who had taught Melany how to control the shadows. He definitely was on her side.

The thought of approaching Medusa and a few

of the other demigods like Achilles and Bellerophon crossed my mind, but I knew there had been bad blood between them and Mel when she basically humiliated them during the mock battle trial.

The last person I checked with before meeting with Jasmine and the others again, was Hecate. Melany had saved her life by getting her out of oblivion. I found her wandering around the shore of the lake just on the edge of the woods. It was where she used to live and where Melany had saved her.

She didn't even look up when I landed on the rocky edge of the water, she just continued to aimlessly pace, looking to the ground, mumbling to herself. Her hair was in tangles and the dress she wore in tatters. She hadn't changed or even showered from weeks ago when Ren had pulled her out of the water. She looked lost, broken. A shell of her former self.

"Hecate?"

Slowly, she lifted her head to look at me, but I wasn't even sure she could see me. It was like she peered right through me to something I couldn't even imagine.

"Melany's in trouble. She's going to need your help."

She hummed, then spoke a few quiet words, going back to plodding along the lakeshore while looking at her feet.

I stood in front of her, and touched her arm so she'd look at me again, see me. Hear me. "I'm sorry for what's happened to you, but Melany really needs your help. She's going to be on trial in two days, can you come and tell everyone how she saved you?"

Hecate's facial expression never changed. Her eyes were glossy, unfocused. I wasn't sure she even heard me. I still had to try. Maybe when she was lucid, she would remember what I asked.

"I know this might be too much to ask, and I don't even know if you understand me, but I need you to find the Furies and tell them to come to the academy. Melany needs them to be there in two days' time."

She murmured something, drool dribbling out between her cracked lips.

My hand dropped, and I let her continue her way. "I'm sorry."

Rising into the sky, I flew back to the academy. Everyone was assembled in the dining hall. Jasmine, Georgina, and Cassandra had gotten almost every recruit from first year on to gather for me. There was a loud rumble in the crowd as I moved through it to the table where Mel, our friends, and I usually sat. I stepped up onto it to address the crowd.

"Thank you for being here. As everyone is aware of, Melany has been wrongfully imprisoned, and a trial is set to be conducted in a couple of days. It's all a bunch of bullshit, but unfortunately, it is being taken seriously by Prometheus. We will need everyone's help to argue in defense of Melany, who we all know has put her life on the line several times for this academy. For all of you. Now it's our turn to risk something for her."

"We're with you, Lucian!" Someone shouted from the crowd.

"Good to hear. What would be the most help is if there is anyone here that witnessed Revana's unfortunate fall. Apollo is trying to spin a lie that Melany was responsible for her death, when we all know it was an accident."

The students looked at each other. A nervous titter spread through the room, and then someone lifted their hand in the air.

It was Mia.

Frowning, Jasmine gaped at her. "You saw what happened?"

Mia nodded.

"Why didn't you ever say anything?"

"Because," she started, then licked her lips nervously, "because I... I didn't want you to be mad at me."

"Why would I be mad at you?"

"What happened, Mia? What did you see?" I urged.

"I saw the ground split open. Melany was on one side and Revana was on the other." She paused again, fiddling with an errant string coming out of the hem of her shirt. "The ground shook again, and Revana fell into the chasm."

I sighed. "Exactly, it wasn't—"

"Melany reached out, grabbing a hold of her hand. She did try and pull her up, but then... then she just let go. And Revana fell to her death."

CHAPTER THIRTEEN

MELANY

I spent two days alone in the detainment cell before anyone came for me. The only other time I saw a person was when one of the guards brought me some food. Greasy meatloaf and stale bread, with water that tasted tinny. Disgusting, but I forced myself to eat and drink. I needed to keep up my strength. Other than the so-called meal delivery, I was by myself.

It sucked. It gave me too much time to think during the day about what I was doing, and too much time to dream at night. Dreams I didn't want to wake from but knew I eventually would. That in itself was a sort of torture.

It took four heavily armed guards to escort me to the Colosseum, where I surmised the sham of a trial was going to take place. Since I wasn't fighting them, they must have assumed that I would flee. Or else, it was a show of power, a way to demonstrate that they'd wrested control over me. As they marched me in, I became aware of a crowd of people sitting up in the seats.

The place was packed. It looked like every single God, demigod, and recruit was there. It reminded me of the day we were rewarded with our blood clans, after going through hell during the twelve trials. That was also the day Hades appeared out of nowhere to claim me as his own.

I pushed the thought out of my mind. I couldn't let myself dwell on the past, not when my very survival depended on what happened in the imme- diate future.

They led me up to the circular stage and told me to sit in the single wooden chair positioned smack dab in the center. It was a rustic setup that looked like it was going to give me splinters. As I sat, I looked out at my accusers.

Apollo and Hera occupied the chairs along one

side of the stage. Beside them were Poseidon, Hermes, and several lower demigods like Achilles and Bellerophon. On the other side, I was relieved to find Hephaistos, Dionysus, Demeter, and Heracles. Beside them stood Lucian, Jasmine, and Georgina. I nearly wept at the sight of them, even though I'd expected them to be there.

Lucian gave me a brave smile. I returned it, imagining that I could feel the energy radiating off of him toward me. Giving me strength. While I sat there and waited for things to start, with everyone staring at me, I could hear some whispers from my peers in the bleachers. I considered just gathering the shadows to me and disappearing, but I suspected that they had the coliseum warded somehow, so I couldn't use my powers on them.

Focusing, I did a little test to see if I was right. I reached out to the darkness, feeling it just hovering at the edges of the stage, but I couldn't bring it any further. They had it blocked or something. Lucian's eyes connected with mine and he gave me a slight head shake. He'd noticed what I was trying to do, and willed me to behave. To cooperate.

When Prometheus stepped up onto the stage, a hush fell over the crowd. "We are gathered here today to answer some questions. Claims have been made, serious claims, that can't be ignored."

"This is all bullshit." I crossed my arms over my chest, and sat back in the chair. My temper rose as I caught the looks being tossed my way. I wasn't sure if I was supposed to be speaking right then or not, but I couldn't help defending myself. "I'm being set up, used as a scapegoat."

That sent a ripple of chaos through the coliseum. It made me feel a bit of grim satisfaction.

Apollo jumped to his feet and pointed at me. "You killed my sister!"

"I didn't kill her! The cave we were in collapsed on her before she could get out! Someone else tried to kill her, and us!"

Prometheus raised his hands. "Please, everyone be quiet. This is not how this is going to work." He gestured to Apollo. "Sit. You will have your turn to talk." He turned to glare at me. "And so will you."

I shook my head. I couldn't believe he was going through with this. Why was he catering to Apollo and Hera? Was he in on their plan to resurrect Zeus? What would he have to gain? With Zeus gone, he'd taken over the running of the academy —like it was originally set up before Zeus threw him and the other Titans into Tartarus for no reason. Except to gain power.

I didn't get it. I didn't see his angle. Plus, my gut said that he wasn't. So then, why was he doing this?

"There have been charges laid against Melany, so we are here to speak to those charges and for Melany to level a defense." He gestured to Apollo, who had anger churning in his eyes and a smug smile on his face. "You may speak now, Apollo."

The golden God stood and walked toward the middle of the stage, where I sat. It was hard, but I resisted the urge to kick him as he passed me.

"A few days ago, Artemis was sent on a search and rescue mission to find Georgina Stewart." He pointed at Georgina, who stood on the side of the arena. She looked uncomfortable at the attention, shifting from foot to foot. "Georgina was supposedly attacked by a white worm, swallowed, and taken to its lair according to Melany and her co-conspirators."

"We are not co-conspirators," Lucian spoke out, frustration heavy in his voice. "There isn't a conspiracy here."

"Well, Melany believes there is in fact a big conspiracy involving the Fates, Thanatos, and our matriarchal leader, Hera, who we all know has suffered greatly since losing her husband and our leader, Zeus. Again, by the hand of this girl." He swung his arm toward me.

That caused some commotion in the stands, whispers and murmurs rising in the air. Some of them I didn't like hearing. Obviously, it wasn't only a few Gods who thought I was some big fat liar. What I didn't understand was what they thought I stood to gain if Apollo's words were true.

"Please stay on topic, Apollo," Prometheus intervened, a bit too late in my opinion. Not that I was going to say anything.

"White worms are not aggressive creatures, so this story was a bit far-fetched to begin with, but Prometheus asked Artemis to check it out, and that is what she did as she was one to follow orders." Apollo lifted his head arrogantly.

I wanted to roll my eyes at the embellishments of his story, but I knew that wouldn't help my case at all, so I refrained, and just continued to glower at him instead.

"Artemis went to the white worms lair and Melany and her friends followed her there. For what purpose, I can't even start to question. They knew she was going to rescue Georgina, her friend, so why would they follow her there?"

He walked the stage like a magician. Sleight of hand. *Look over here, while I feed you a bunch of bullshit lies.*

"I had a vision in which I saw my sister being suffocated by dark power. Powers that only Melany possesses now that Hades is gone. When they returned to the academy with their friend, Melany told me that the cave collapsed, and that was how Artemis died. That is a bald face lie. My sister was a great warrior, strong. A few tons of rock and dirt wouldn't be able to kill her. So, she had to have already been dead before the cave-in."

There were more than a few leaps of logic in his story, but I didn't have the chance to tell him that.

"Melany killed Artemis!" He swung around and pointed at me. "Of that I have no doubt in my mind."

A wave of shocked gasps surged through the coliseum. If this had been a real trial, in front of a jury of my peers, I could already predict the verdict. Guilty as hell.

Georgina stepped forward. She was shaking, she was so upset. Her skin flushed red, and her voice trembled with rage. "You are lying. There was someone else in that cave. Melany didn't try to kill Artemis with her power. After we got out, she wanted to go back and help Artemis but the ground sunk in front of us."

"I had a vision, girl. I saw it. My visions are never wrong," Apollo assured, like someone not accustomed to being questioned.

"She never used her powers on her—"

"Then who did? Tell me that, huh? Who else possesses dark power like that?" His voice was smug, reflecting his absolute certainty.

"I don't know, but it wasn't Melany." Tears escaped her eyes, effortlessly rolling down her cheeks, and it tore me apart to see them there. She'd been inside one of those giant worms, kidnapped and dragged into the bowels of the earth. She'd suffered enough, couldn't anybody see that?

I bolted to my feet. I'd had enough. "This sham is over. I'm not going to sit here and defend myself against things I didn't do."

Barely resisting the urge to bare my teeth at him like a feral animal, I glowered at Apollo.

"I didn't kill your sister. I'm sad she's dead, but it wasn't by my hand. And I didn't kill Hades to take his power, that's just hurtful to hear. Now, Zeus, I killed but in self-defense. He was going to kill me. He was going to slaughter all of you." I swung my arm around the stage to include Gods, demigods and recruits. "If he'd had his way, you'd all be dead so he could gain more power. So, you're welcome! You should be kissing my ass…"

"She killed Revana!" A voice I didn't recognize shouted.

I spun around to the bleachers, to find a boy I didn't know standing there, making the accusation. Who was he? "What did you say? Who told you that?"

"Mia did!" He turned to look over at Mia, who wasn't on the stage beside Jasmine but in the crowd with everyone else. That wasn't right. It couldn't be. "She said she saw you deliberately drop Revana in the chasm."

What the hell?! Why on earth would she say that?

Before I could respond, there was a loud pounding at the one of the closed doors. The sound echoed throughout the coliseum. It came again, making some people jump and others murmur nervously, then the doors slammed open and a form with golden wings zipped into the space like a giant bee.

My heart leapt into my throat and I gasped.

It was Artemis.

She flew around the room, looking confused and upset. I studied her as she moved. The toga she always wore was torn and shredded in some places, specked with dirt. Her blond curly hair was dirty and in disarray surrounding her face. A face marred by flecks of soil, and a few small cuts.

A storm of emotion raged in her eyes, and yet, there was also a blankness. The lights were on, but I wasn't sure that anyone was home.

"Sister!" Apollo shouted at her, spreading his arms wide for an embrace. "You're alive. I'm so happy to see you. We all thought you were dead."

She didn't respond to his comments, or to his voice. Instead, she continued to gawk all around her, her gaze flitting from person to person. It looked like she didn't recognize anyone. Her confusion was evident in every jerky movement she made.

"Artemis?" Apollo called after her, starting to notice that she wasn't acting normal. "What's going on?" He unfurled his wings and rose into the air next to her. It was like approaching an injured bird. A very dangerous bird with a sword.

Unsheathing her blade, she swung it at him, making a grunting sound deep in her throat. Luckily, Apollo was quick, and he was able to duck from her swing, flying backward to give her space.

"What the hell is wrong with her?" he shouted down to us.

"She's dead," I spoke the words flatly, listening to the ripple of gasps and shocked murmurs spreading through the room.

Frowning, Apollo floated down toward me. I cast him a glower that I hoped conveyed that I wasn't interested in him getting too close to me. "What do you mean she's dead? She's right here in front of us."

Lucian and the others came to stand around me in a half-circle of protection, and I felt myself grow stronger with the people I trusted at my back. Prometheus also came to my side. So, now he was starting to believe me? I wanted to say that I told him so.

"I told you that Death was gone. This is the result."

Before I could explain further, more guards rushed into the auditorium. One of them ran up onto the stage, heading toward Prometheus. He was pale, his expression dismayed. "Sir. We've had a distress call from Pecunia."

"What is it? What's going on?"

The guard swallowed. "They said the dead have risen, and they are eating people."

CHAPTER FOURTEEN

MELANY

*C*ommotion swept the coliseum as the news spread about the dead rising in Pecunia. I heard a few frightened gasps, and at least one person started crying. I was sure it the was the boy who had accused me of killing Revana.

Trying to restore order, Prometheus raised his hands. "Everyone calm down. First years, please return to your dorm rooms. Second years please return to your hall. Everyone else remain here so we can coordinate a response to the distress call."

"What should we do about her?" Dionysus gestured to Artemis, who was still flying around erratically and swinging her sword at anyone who tried to get near her, which presently included Apollo and Hermes.

Prometheus grabbed one of the guards nearby. "Get the net."

While they tried to figure out how to contain a dead Goddess, I huddled with Lucian, Jasmine, and Georgina, frowning at Jasmine. "What's going on with Mia? Why would she say that shit?"

"I don't know." She shrugged. "When she first said it, I asked her, but she didn't really give me an answer."

"It's bullshit. You all know that, right?" My eyes connected with each of them, gauging their reaction.

"Of course we know that," Lucian replied.

"Do you think someone got to her?" I asked. "She is in Hera's blood clan."

Jasmine turned to look over at the bleachers where the third years were—those who had fought before—to find Mia sitting, arms wrapped around her chest. She wasn't looking at anything but the floor. She did look lost, though. She even looked defeated.

I was angry at her, but maybe she had a reason for saying what she did, and I would reserve my judgement until we found out the truth.

"I'll go talk to her." Jasmine walked down the few steps from the stage, joining her girlfriend in the seats. She sat down beside her, but Mia didn't look at her.

My attention got nabbed when the guard returned with a huge net made with golden thread.

"Clear the stage," Prometheus ordered, waving his hands at everyone.

We all stepped down, as three guards dragged the net to the center of the floor. Apollo landed next to it to inspect it.

"It won't hurt her, will it?" he questioned.

I thought about reminding him that she was dead, but thought that might be a bit insensitive considering the circumstances, so I kept my mouth shut.

He spun around to glare at me anyway—as if he'd read my thoughts—and picked up the edge of the net while Hermes and a guard grabbed the others. Lifting it into the air, they flew toward Artemis and cornered her. The goddess lashed out at them like a wild animal, but they threw the net on top of her.

Artemis thrashed about, using her hands and

sword to try to cut the line, but it had obviously been made of unbreakable threads, and her movements only helped to secure it around her even tighter. Carefully, they brought her back down to the stage.

"Now what do we do with her?" Hermes asked Prometheus.

"We should probably secure her in one of the cells until we can solve this situation." He looked over at me. "Ideas?"

"You're asking me? That's pretty bold of you." I knew I was being facetious, but I was tired of being treated like a criminal in one hand and a savior in the other.

"This doesn't change anything," Apollo spat. "She should still be on trial for murder. We should throw her in the same cell as Artemis and see how they get along."

"We're going to need all hands on deck for this," Prometheus argued.

"Are you going to throw me in a cell after I lead the charge on this?"

Prometheus kept my gaze. "It's possible."

I thought about just escaping. I could easily, everyone was preoccupied, but I also knew that the army was going to need me if we were going to contain the situation. Lucian gave me a look that said he suspected what I was considering and he didn't approve.

I sighed. Sometimes being a hero sucked.

"I suppose we're going to need a lot of nets. There are over a thousand graves in Pecunia alone."

A half hour later, thirty recruits from the Demigods Academy, including Lucian, Jasmine, Georgina, Mia, and I, crossed the oceanic portal to Cala to battle the dead. Others like Diego and Cassandra came with us as well, despite her not having wings. She had insisted on helping, and since she'd developed a very cool light power that I'd seen her use in Tartarus, and then again aiding me to escape Hera, we welcomed her. Medusa and a handful of demigods also joined us, along with a few Gods.

After emerging from the water, we took to the sky and flew to Pecunia. As we glided over the sparsely populated village, before reaching the city, a group of shambling forms dotted the land. It didn't take long to realize those forms were people back from the dead, having dug themselves out of some shallow grave somewhere. We ignored those since they seemed not to be a danger to anyone, but the closer we got to the city, the more the dead began to attack.

I pointed out a small group of shambling undead who had cornered a frantic looking woman and her little girl. "I'll take care of that."

Lucian nodded. "I'll go with you."

The two of us swooped down toward the pack of previously deceased that were reaching for the woman and girl, who had hoisted themselves up onto the roof of an SUV. Thankfully, it didn't seem like any of them could climb. Their hands reached and missed over and over again, groaning every now and then.

Without slowing down, Lucian picked up the woman while I scooped up the girl, flying them a block away to a quiet residential street so they could seek shelter. They thanked us and the little girl hugged my legs so tightly that I thought they were going to snap, then ran to a house whose owner had opened the door and beckoned them inside to safety.

Once they were safe, we returned to the small pack of zombies. Landing on top of the building nearby, we wondered what we were going to do about them. Most of the bodies were pretty decayed—dead probably for a few years—some were missing limbs, others had skeletal arms, and one guy limped on a skinless leg. If it wasn't so horrifying in principal, I was pretty sure I would've laughed.

"What do we do with them?" I asked.

Below us, the dead had gathered, reaching up toward the roof.

Glancing around, Lucian's gaze landed on the cars parked in the lot, then his eyes narrowed. "This is an auto repair shop. We could open the bay door, lead them inside, and then lock them up."

I nodded. "Yeah, that'll work."

After we secured the small mob of zombies, we caught up with the rest of the group near the city center, where most of the problem seemed to concentrate. Someone had already deployed one giant net that captured a group of about thirty bodies. Unfortunately, there were a few casualties, and it seemed like three people suffered from scratches and bite marks. Thankfully, they were being treated by Chiron, who had accompanied us for that very reason.

Lucian and I landed next to Jasmine and Georgina, who were trying to shepherd living people into a safe place.

"How's it going?" I asked them.

"This is the craziest thing I think we've ever faced." Jasmine shook her head.

"I don't know, I'd say the chimera was pretty crazy, and so was the typhon." I chuckled.

When I heard the dead were rising, I thought about the chimera immediately. I was very happy that the Furies had taken the body after we killed it, chopped it up and ate it as a delicacy. I'd never been so thankful for their grotesque eating habits. The last thing we needed was some half-crazed, three-headed monster showing up to devour people. Not to mention that if it was already dead, we'd really have a hard time killing it again.

For the next few hours, we rounded up the walking deceased in nets, and fenced areas and in empty buildings with good locks. Some of the residents of Pecunia suffered mild injuries from running, and a few unlucky ones experienced more bites and scratches. Unfortunately, one young man had a big chunk of his leg torn out before we were able to get to him, but Chiron managed to stitch him up and put one of Dionysus's healing concoctions on it. The guy would keep his leg, thankfully.

I took to the air and did a reconnaissance flight along the surrounding neighborhoods, to make sure we'd rounded up all of them. Curious, I flew over the community I used to live in with the Demos. Their house wasn't there anymore, the estate had been destroyed in the earthquake created by a cyclopes under the power of Aphrodite and her golden rope. It was just leveled ground now.

It looked like it was getting ready for another estate to be built on the land, and I wondered if the Demos were the ones rebuilding. I'd forgotten to ask Callie and Mrs. Demos when I saw them a while back.

Slowly descending, I landed on the space where the cottage I previously lived in had stood. I walked around the area, kicking at the loose stones on the ground. There had been big oak trees there, lilac bushes, and a beautifully landscaped garden with a fountain and cobblestone paths.

I'd spent many days and nights running over the grounds, mostly running away from my responsibilities, trying to escape from my life here. A life that had felt stifling and strange, and not mine. What I wouldn't give to have that back for just a few hours. I would give anything to see Sophia again and feel her hands on mine, smelling the vanilla scent she always seemed to carry on her skin.

It felt like a lifetime ago since I was last here, not

just a mere three years.

When I turned to leave, movement out of the corner of my eye drew my attention. I swung back around to see someone shuffling across the dirt lot toward me, and I drew in a sharp breath. I recognized the blue flowered dress she wore, and the dark strands of hair—mere whisps now—on top of her head.

My legs felt like jelly, and my knees nearly gave out the closer she got to me, but I didn't dare move. I couldn't. She kept shuffling toward me, one foot missing a shoe—her good temple shoes if I wasn't mistaken—causing her to list to one side with each step.

I held my breath until she was right in front of me. Her head rose, wispy dark strands stuck to her hollowed out cheeks, and I stared into brown eyes, opaque from the erosion of time. Her mouth opened, cracked lips ripping even more, and she let out a long, low groan.

Tears sprung from my eyes, until there was a deluge down my cheeks. I reached for her, cupping her decaying face with my hands. She tried to snap at my fingers with broken browned teeth, but I held her head firmly.

"Sophia. Oh Gods, Sophia."

CHAPTER FIFTEEN

MELANY

My broken heart shattered a little bit more as I stared into the decaying face of my mother.

"I've missed you," I croaked, my throat tightening from the flood of emotions flowing through me.

Sophia groaned again, pushing forward, snapping her jaws on a type of autopilot, but I knew it wasn't in response to what I'd said. Beyond any real sense of consciousness, she couldn't really see or hear me, her daughter. She was just a shell of a person. There was no soul inside her now.

My Sophia, the woman who adopted me after my parents died in a car crash, and raised me as her own, was gone, killed in the earthquake that leveled the Demos's estate. There was nothing that could change that fact.

Releasing my hold on her face, I took a step backward. She stumbled forward, trying to grab me with a swipe of her rotting fingers, but I easily dodged out of the way. My feet took another few steps away from her, and I watched her for another few seconds. Feeling too raw, I unfurled my wings and took to the sky once more.

I left her there, stumbling around, lost. She wasn't a threat to anyone. There was no one in the vicinity she could possibly hurt, so I flew back to the town center. When I touched down near the statue that had been erected for us in tribute, I found Lucian and the others. It looked like they'd contained the situation.

"Where did you go?" Lucian set his hand on my arm, in that gentle way of his.

"I went to my old neighborhood."

"Are you okay?"

"There was nothing there." I didn't elaborate.

His gaze searched my eyes, probably seeing that

they were red and swollen from my tears, but he didn't press me for details.

Prometheus joined us then. "It looks like all the dead have been rounded up. Now we just need Thanatos to come back." He gave me a pointed look.

"Why are you staring at me?"

"Because you're the only person I've known in a thousand years, who has spoken to Death and lived to talk about it."

"What do you think I'm going to do, ask nicely and he'll just pop back to solve this shit?"

Before Prometheus could respond, a loud screech reverberated from the sky. Everyone looked up, curious and scared. My stomach roiled when I recognized that sound. I'd heard it before, and I wasn't the only one.

Lucian and I shared a look. He, too, remembered that screech echoing off the craggy mountains of Tartarus.

A huge ice-blue dragon crested over the hill, swooping down toward the town center. As it neared, I could see two figures riding on its back. There was no mistaking the golden hair, although most of it was missing, Aphrodite.

"Holy shit!" Jasmine shouted, and I most definitely shared her distressed shock.

For a split second, there was an unsettling, eerie silence that filled the square as everyone's heads tilted up, and they stared wide-eyed at the encroaching horror. I could hear every heart beat, every intake of air from the people around me, while we all held our breaths in anticipation.

A scream suddenly split the air, breaking the spell, and chaos reigned down upon us.

Everybody scattered when Khione sprayed a stream of ice through the plaza, demolishing the mall that had been erected. Bits of stone and wood went flying everywhere. A piece of wood hit my boot, puncturing the leather while I dashed out of the way alongside Lucian and Jasmine. We ended up huddling just outside a pizza joint, under the awning with a few civilians, Prometheus and Chiron.

"What do we do?" Jasmine asked.

"Fight them off, protect the people, and try and not to die. Although, I guess today would be an okay day for that, since it won't stick."

"And you wonder why I called you reckless," Prometheus grumbled.

"Do you have a better idea?" I challenged. Not

waiting for his response, I stepped out from under the awning, Lucian and Jasmine followed.

"We need to take Khione down. She's causing the most damage," Lucian concluded, assessing the destroyed square while the dragon flew around for a second attack.

"What do you suggest?" Jasmine questioned, following his gaze.

"Cutting off her head would do it," I answered simply.

Jasmine shuddered. "That's gruesome."

"Agreed, but she's already dead. She's not going to feel it. Khione's beyond that. Once Aphrodite and Ares are on the ground, we should be able to neutralize their attacks."

"Maybe we should cut their heads off too," Lucian offered, but I knew he'd said it sarcastically.

"Not a terrible idea."

"I was joking."

"I know." Smirking, I took to the sky.

Once we were all up, I looked around to spot the others. We'd need everyone on this. I spied Bellerophon and Medusa taking a breather near the park. They were actually lounging on one of the benches, but they weren't going to get a pass on this one.

"We need Medusa on this," I called to Jasmine and Lucian before swooping down to toward them.

When I touched down, Bellerophon, outfitted in his usual black armor, jumped to his feet and immediately took up a defensive position with his sword.

"Relax," I snickered. "I'm not going to kill you." I was joking, sort of, since everyone thought I was some villainous God killer now.

Medusa snorted. She obviously liked my joke.

A roar came from above and we all looked up as Khione made another pass over the town center, a new stream of ice erupting from her. Luckily, it did nothing but flash freeze a few cars parked on the street, because Georgina, Cassandra, and the other recruits, had gotten all the civilians off the roads and into the safety of the surrounding buildings.

"More victims of yours, Melany?" Medusa gestured to the dragon and the two Gods riding on her back.

"If you must know, Khione attacked Aphrodite and I tried to save her, but I was too late."

"What about Ares?"

"He tried to kill me, and I defended myself."

I gave Lucian a look. He'd left out the part of Cassandra actually giving the killing blow to Ares. He was protecting her, and I respected that.

"And then the mountain came down on all of them," I explained.

Snorting, Medusa shook her head, all one hundred of her tiny snake hairs hissed in my direction. "So, really, the only person you've actually killed is Zeus?"

"Yup. And he deserved it." I wouldn't let anyone make me feel guilty about destroying the God of Lightning and Thunder. I'd done it to protect everyone who was important to me. I'd done it to avenge Hades.

"I'm trying to decide if I believe you or not," she retorted.

"I really don't care if you do. Right now, we have a bigger problem, and we need to take care of it."

Medusa shrugged, briefly glancing at Bellerophon. "What do you want us to do?"

"Once we take down Khione, I need you to get close enough to Ares and Aphrodite, and turn them to stone. It's the only way to stop them for good."

"All right, I guess I can do that. I can add them to my collection in the maze."

A mischievous glint illuminated her features. There were rumors and whispers about her in the academy too. They said that all the statues in the maze were once her lovers, who had disappointed her so she turned them to stone. She understood the power of gossip; it could easily make you either a hero or a villain…

Or if you were really lucky, a legend.

Before we took off, Georgina and Cassandra ran across the road to meet us. "What's the plan?" Georgina asked.

After swiftly filling her in, she agreed to stay on the ground with Cassandra, protecting the towns-people. Lucian, Jasmine, and I flew up and hovered over the square, waiting for Khione to make another round, which seemed to be her pattern.

It made me wonder if the dragon was acting solely on instinct. Although, I believed something had made them come here, just like when I found Sophia at the house where she once lived. Even in death, there was something compelling them to do the things they were doing. Maybe the level of instinct and compulsion depended on how long they had been gone.

It wasn't long before we heard the thwack of large leathery wings flapping in the sky. Khione swooped over the plaza again with an ear-piercing screech that sent a shiver down my back. We each pulled our swords from their scabbards on our belts, and positioned ourselves apart in a triangle formation.

I hoped that she was just on autopilot, and spewed ice across the square, so we could fly toward her after that, without having to worry whether she would sprays us or not. Opening her giant jaws, her icy breath erupted from her, cutting a line across the ground again. The second she closed her mouth, I zoomed toward her, sword at the ready. Lifting it over my head, I prepared to bring it down across her neck, when her head suddenly turned to look at me. Her mouth opened, and she shot at me.

Shit. I'd miscalculated the situation.

Thankfully, I was agile enough to dodge the icy bolt. With Khione's attention on me, Lucian and Jasmine were able to get close and swing at her neck. They both landed solid blows that severed muscles and tendons along her throat. Her head drooped, hanging by only a few ribbons of flesh and some bone.

I was about to let out a triumphant whoop, but shouted instead when I saw Ares swing the large spear he'd been holding at Lucian. The tip plunged through Lucian's ribs and he was catapulted to the side, spiraling to the ground as he tried to regain control.

Immidiately, I shot toward him, but by the time I reached him he'd pulled out of the spear, and hovered a few feet from the street. Blood stained his shirt, dribbling through his fingers while a hand pressed against the wound along his right side.

"You good?"

He nodded, but I could see he was in pain.

"Find Chiron. Get fixed up."

"I can still—"

I shook my head. "You're too important. Jas and I got this."

"Are you sure?"

"Yes." I gave him a small smile.

After he flew over to the pizza joint where we'd left Chiron and Prometheus, I moved up to Jasmine, who waited nearby.

"I'm going to distract it again, and you finish the job. But watch out for Ares."

She nodded, then soared back up to position herself. I did the same, just as Khione swung back around for another fly over of the plaza—her head hanging grotesquely from her neck. As she passed by, she opened her mouth but nothing came out. We must've severed the tubes that carried her power from where she generated it inside her body.

I flew in front of her anyway, to get her attention. She tried to turn toward me but I could see her struggle. Jasmine came at her from the other side, and brought her sword down, finally severing her head.

Khione immediately dropped to the ground. When she landed in a earth-shaking thud, Aphrodite and Ares were thrown from her back.

From where I hovered, I spotted Medusa and Bellerophon running toward the downed dragon. Ares had already recovered from the fall, and was up and marching toward them, his spear ready at his side. To be honest, he didn't look or act much differently than he had when he was alive.

Reaching him first, Bellerophon blocked the blow of Ares' weapon, then swung his blade, slicing off the God's arm. Although, that didn't seem to stop him from attacking the black knight again. Medusa rushed to him, took off her glasses, and focusing on him, she turned him to stone.

I'd never seen the process before, so I assumed it would be an immediate transformation, but it wasn't. It was like flash freezing, except with stone instead of ice. Starting at his feet, his flesh turned white, hardening into the mineral cell by cell, then it spread over his whole body until it enclosed his head. He was a statue, forever frozen mid action.

It was unsettling.

Not waiting to watch her do the same thing to Aphrodite, I dove back down to land near the pizza place, only to witness the commotion. I heard Jasmine's cries before I saw her, and ran the rest of the way. Pushing a few recruits aside, who had gathered under the now frayed and torn awning, I found Jasmine, Lucian and Cassandra surrounding Mia who was up on a table being worked on by Chiron.

"What happened?!"

Jasmine gestured to her girlfriend's stomach. There was a hole in it, ice crystals forming along the edges. Instantly, I realized what happened to the awning. The last beam of ice from Khione must have broken through it, piercing Mia before she could jump away.

When Mia saw me, she lifted a hand toward me. I took it. "I'm sorry, Mel. I shouldn't have said those things." She coughed, her whole body shaking from the effort.

"Don't talk, Mia. Save your strength."

"Hera threatened me... she was going to expel me and go after my family..." She coughed again, and blood seeped between her lips.

Gently shushing her, Jasmine wiped it away.

Tears ran down her cheeks, and my heart ached for her.

As Chiron used his healing power on Mia, I noticed that Lucian's wound had thankfully been patched up and bandaged also by Chiron I imagined.

While I watched Chiron, and heard Jasmine's pleas for Mia to hold on, I felt a bit of a disconnect. Out of the corner of my eye, I swore I saw the shadows undulate and shimmer, so I turned toward them and stared, certain I spied someone moving inside the darkness. I knew who was there.

Reaching out, I pulled the shadows toward me, yanking the being inside them as well, until I was completely shrouded in the darkness—removed from what was going on outside of it.

"Fancy seeing you here, Thanatos." I narrowed my eyes at Death.

"Hello, Melany."

"What are you doing here?"

"Waiting."

"For what?"

Through the veil of shadows, he lifted his skeletal hand, gesturing to Mia.

"Why her? Why now, when you've let everything else go to hell?"

"I have my orders."

"Where are the Fates? Are they with you?"

"I can't tell you where, but they are safely sleeping."

"You can't have Mia," I challenged. "I won't let you take her."

Still, he didn't say anything, and it was equal parts maddening and unnerving.

"You can have me."

He turned his hooded head toward me. It was completely black inside the hood, but I knew he was looking at me. His gaze, if he had eyes, boring right through me to my very core.

"You would sacrifice yourself for this girl?"

"It's not just Mia I'm doing this for. It's for all of them. When the time is right, you can come and take me. But I get to choose the when and where. Deal?"

"Yes, we have a deal." With the ominous words, he started to fade back into the shadows.

"Before you go, do the right thing. There are a lot of dead people walking around who shouldn't be here. That's your fault."

"Very well." Lifting his hand, he snapped his skeletal fingers. Then he was gone, and I was back to standing under the torn awning with everyone else.

My attention returned to Chiron. "How is she?"

He gave me a stunned look. "She'll live. I don't know what happened, but her stomach is healing on its own."

"Good."

Frowning, Lucian came to my side. "Where did you go? You were here one second and the next you vanished."

"I took care of the situation."

"What does that mean?"

Without answering, I gestured to the section of the park where we'd fenced in a group of dead. They were all back on the ground, unmoving.

"You saw Death."

I nodded. "And now I'm pretty sure I know where the Fates are."

CHAPTER SIXTEEN

MELANY

*A*fter we helped the people of Pecunia return their dead to their proper burial spots, we went back to the academy. I was hesitant as to what kind of welcome I was going to receive, and whether or not Prometheus was just going to toss my ass back into a cell. I could've left. No one was stopping me, but I owed it to my friends to go back with them to make sure they were okay.

The moment I went through the main doors, Apollo and Hera appeared, demanding that my prosecution be reconvened.

"Melany will not be back on trial. She has been

exonerated," Prometheus announced, shocking us all with his change of heart.

"By who?!" Apollo raged.

"By me." The titan seemed to grow another foot as he stared Apollo down, until the God swallowed and took a step back.

Apollo's furious glare focused on me. "I won't ever forget this. It isn't over between you and me."

"Whatever." I shrugged.

He didn't like that response at all, and I thought he was going to explode right there and then, but Hera intervened. Setting her hand on his shoulder, she leaned down and whispered something in his ear. It must've been satisfactory to him for the moment, as he turned and walked away. Hera smirked at me, following him.

I had no doubt that Hera had something major planned, and I needed to be ready.

After that little scene, I went to the infirmary to check on Mia and Ren. When I arrived, everyone else was already there. My gaze found Lucian and Cassandra in a deep discussion with Chiron, while Jasmine sat with Mia, who was healing quickly. Georgina was at Ren's bed, holding his hand. It looked like he was finally on the mend.

This place of healing had become a sort of

sanctuary for us. Or it could have been that one of us always seemed to be in here, recuperating from one injury or another.

I joined Mia and Jasmine first. The instant Jasmine saw me, she stood, hugging me tightly. "I know you had something to do with her healing. Thank you."

When I pulled back, Mia grabbed my hand. "I told Prometheus the truth."

"Yeah, I figured since he didn't lock me up."

"I'm sorry, I—" Her voice cracked.

"It's okay. I understand wanting to protect your family."

Leaving them to convalescence together, I joined Georgina and Ren. He looked lucid and gave me a smile. "I'm sorry I missed all the excitement."

"Oh, I'm sure there will be another battle for you to join in soon enough."

His eyes narrowed. "That sounds like a warning."

I shrugged. "Nah, just a prediction. We're always fighting this or that. It's our job now."

"I see you're in one piece," Lucian said, coming over to our side with Cassandra.

"Yup. Prometheus wouldn't let Apollo rip me limb from limb, so that's good."

A chuckle escaped him. "You said something about the Fates. That you know where they are?"

Sighing, I nodded. "I'm pretty sure they're tucked away in the most obvious place. A place I've already been to."

"Where?"

"I'll tell everyone later. Right now, I think we could all use some downtime." Feeling the tension on my shoulders, I rolled them. "I could do with a good flight though. Burn off some of this energy. Want to join me?"

"Yeah. We haven't gone flying in a while."

Once we were outside, we both stretched out our wings, then slowly rose into the air together. Soon we were flying over the academy and grounds, weaving in and around each other, as we'd done in the past. I took off, and Lucian chased me. It had been a long time since we'd played around as if we didn't have a care in the world.

I couldn't remember the last moment that I felt like the world and all of its problems weren't sitting on my shoulders.

We played chase and tag for over an hour. By the time we landed on the shore of the lake to take a break, every muscle in my body ached. It was a good ache. The one that told you, you were alive and well, healthy.

Lucian picked up a flat stone from the ground. "I bet I can skip it five times."

"You're on. What do I win if you can't?"

"What do you want?"

My face scrunched up, thinking about the most embarrassing thing I could make him do. "I want you to stand up on the table during dinner, and sign Justin Timberlake's 'Sexy Back'."

Lucian laughed. "No way."

"I bet you have a great singing voice."

"You'd bet wrong then."

Grabbing a flat stone, I fired it across the lake. It bounced four times then sunk. I turned and gave him a little curtsy. "Beat that if you can."

I watched Lucian step up to the edge of the lake, the sunlight glinting off the gold in his hair, giving him the most breathtaking glow, and felt a pang of regret in my gut. I wished we could have more of these times together. Simple. No expectations. Just a chance to be ourselves, without pretense. Without the weight of our past decisions pressing down on us.

I wanted to be free of that. I wanted Lucian to be free of me.

He let the rock go, and it skipped across the water, once, twice, three times, then four… and a fifth time. Pumping his fist into the air, he let out a loud whoop.

"Ha! In your face." His laughter danced around us.

"Good job." I raised my hand for a high-five and he slapped it, intertwining his fingers with mine and lowering our joined hands.

His smile disappeared as he tugged me a little closer to him. He looked me in the eyes, and I didn't shy away. We stood like that, staring at each other while the breeze blew around us, and the waves of the lake lapped against the shore. Birds chirped from nearby trees. It was a perfect moment. Frozen in time forever.

The way he held my hand and the way he gazed into my eyes, as if forever memorizing me, told me he knew why I'd brought us here to the lake. The place where we'd first made love.

My hand lifted to his face, cupping his cheek. "You are the most loving, compassionate, heroic man I've ever known. I've been so lucky to know you, like I have. You will always have a piece of my heart and soul to the day I die."

He covered my hand with his. "Why do I get the sense that you're saying goodbye, *goodbye*, and not just breaking up with me?"

"I'm freeing you, Lucian. You know it's the right thing."

His gaze searched mine for a long moment, while he bit his bottom lip. "I know."

"I love you, but not in the way you deserve."

"I love you too, but I guess not in the way you want."

Slowly, he lowered his hand, and mine dropped too. Wrapping my arms around him, I hugged him close, feeling him reciprocate. With a sigh, kissed the side of my head and let go.

When we pulled apart, I gave him a wry smile. "I'm pretty sure Cassandra is in love with you."

"I know," he said with a bit of a shy lift to his shoulders.

"She's pretty cool. I like her. She ain't no Melany Richmond, but hey?" I gave an exaggerated shrug that made him laugh.

"Your ego is a force all on its own."

I doubled over, laughing hard.

After the bittersweet flight back to the academy, Lucian excused himself, saying he had a job to do with Heracles before we entered the main doors, and he flew in another direction—toward the west training fields. I didn't know if that was true, or an excuse, but I couldn't' blame him for it. It wasn't going to be easy between us now that the deed was done, and we'd both need time.

The second I stepped inside the school, I knew who I wanted to see and to talk to next. I made a pit stop at Dionysus's office, as he had all the good junk food stashed away in his cupboards. Once I took a few bags of chips, some gummy bears and a huge bar of chocolate, I strode through the corridors to Demeter's Hall, out the back and into the garden where I knew I'd find Georgina digging away in the dirt.

When she looked up, the surprise on her face was comical. "What are you doing here?"

I tossed down all the snacks and folded my legs down on a patch of grass next to her. "Thought we could use some good food for a change. I'm getting tired of protein bars and power smoothies."

She gave me a challenging look. "That's not what you eat, Mel. You happily gorge on pancakes, fruit, and whipped cream every morning."

"Okay, but it's what you eat. So, I thought you could use some fun food for a change." Tearing open the chocolate bar, I snapped off half, and handed it to her.

Gina shoved the whole thing in her mouth, her eyes rolling back in supreme pleasure as she chewed. I bit off a piece and let it melt in my mouth, enjoying the way it tasted on my tongue. It was funny what a person found pleasure after months and months of pain and suffering.

After I finished the chocolate, I laid back on the patch of grass, closed my eyes, and soaked up the sunlight that streamed down on me.

"What's going on, Mel?"

I pried open one eye to peek at Georgina as she stared at me. "I'm trying to enjoy the day. You should be doing the same." My hand reached for her metal arm, pulling her down to the ground with me. The patch of grass was small, so we had to huddle together to fit. Which was fine by me.

A long sigh escaped her, and I wondered how long it had been since she'd taken a day to relax. I honestly couldn't remember the last time I did since being here. Maybe it had been with Lucian during our first year, maybe it had been with Hades during my training. It didn't really matter.

"This is my favorite spot," Georgina confessed. "I feel good when I'm here."

I turned onto my side so I could look at her. "Promise me you'll take more time for yourself."

Her head turned to me, brow furrowing. "Mel, I don't like it when you talk like this."

"It's fine. Everything's fine." I slung my arm around her. "Let's just lay here for a bit, okay? Before everything gets complicated again."

"Okay."

Snuggling closer to her, I rested my head against her shoulder and closed my eyes. Sunrays warmed my skin, and I let my body relax. For the next few minutes, or an hour, or more, I wasn't going to think about the future. Think about what I had to do and what it was going to cost to do it. I was just going to lay there next to my best friend and let the sun melt away every problem, every care.

I was just going to be Melany, a rebellious girl with blue-hair, and a penchant for pancakes... not a demigod who was going to save the world. Again.

CHAPTER SEVENTEEN

MELANY

*D*inner in the dining hall was a somber affair. I supposed everyone felt like there was something hanging over us. Something that had to be done.

I picked at my food, despite it being pizza—my favorite. Sitting on the opposite side of the table, Lucian watched me now and then, but I looked up to catch him, he'd look away. This was our first time together after our rendezvous at the lake. The tension was palpable, and I suspected everyone felt it.

After we'd eaten and the dining hall cleared of

recruits, I asked Jasmine, Georgina, Lucian and Cassandra to meet me in the maze, away from prying eyes and curious ears—Mia and Ren were still laid up in the infirmary. Basically, I just didn't want Hera to catch wind of our meeting.

Flying down to the center of the labyrinth, I found the others already there, waiting.

"This is about the Fates?" Lucian asked.

I nodded. "They're in the Temple of Night."

"How do you know?" Jasmine asked.

"It's something Thanatos said when I saw him in Pecunia. I think Nyx is the one pulling the strings."

"Why would Nyx want to resurrect Zeus?"

"I don't know, but we're going to find out."

"How?"

"We're going to sneak into the Temple of Night."

"And how are we going to do that?" Jasmine asked.

"Through our dreams."

There was movement in the bushes, and a form moved out of the darkness, carrying a torch. The firelight illuminated Hecate's face as she approached us.

"Hecate's going to help us summon Hypnos, and we're going to convince him to help us in."

Lucian grabbed my arm and pulled me off to the side. "The last time I saw Hecate she was an incoherent zombie wandering the lake's shore. She looked like she hadn't showered in weeks. At least it looks like she combed her hair. Besides that, I couldn't get two words out of her, now she's helping us?"

"You're right, Lucian, I was lost," Hecate answered. "Something happened to my memories when I crossed over with Melany, they were confused and jumbled. But everything came back to me. Every memory, every hurt, every moment of love. It's that love I'm banking on."

"Why would Hypnos help us?" Lucian asked.

"Because he and Hecate were once lovers, and Nyx destroyed their relationship. I'm hoping he wants some payback," I explained

To summon Hypnos, Hecate had us lay on the ground toe to head in a pentagon. She sat in the center with her torch and sprigs of juniper. Burning it would put us in a relaxed state, like being drugged, just on the edge of sleep. The witch mentioned Hypnos and his dream creatures would come for us, and when he was almost upon us, she would nudge me awake so we could have a little chat.

Despite everything that had happened in oblivion, I trusted Hecate, even when the others didn't. I knew what she'd been through, what Nyx had done to her when she snapped her out of existence because she didn't like it that Hecate was having a relationship with her son Hypnos.

Following Hecate's instructions, we took a few deep breaths while she burned the juniper over the torch flame. The air instantly filled with the woodsy cedar-like smell, and I closed my eyes trying to relax. Inhaling the smoke with another deep breath, my body instantly melted into the ground, every muscle going limp and lax. I felt floaty, almost like I'd been drugged. It wasn't entirely unpleasant, and I stifled the giggles that were trying to erupt inside me at the most inappropriate moment.

Soon, I was deep under the thrall of darkness and I felt sleep just a blink away. I could hear a scratching sound that I didn't like, and the vibration of something flapping around my face sent a shiver down my body. Hecate pinched my toe and my eyes snapped open.

Suddenly, I was face to face with tiny, glowing red eyes, and a leathery black face of some kind of feline-like, demonic creature with bat wings. It hissed at me when it noticed I was awake, and not asleep as it had thought.

Glancing up, I found Hypnos clad in a long black robe, his dream creatures sitting on his shoulders, and one perched on top of his head. His hollow face was turned toward Hecate, and if he had features, I suspected they would've been twisted into a mask of surprise at seeing his old lover.

"Hecate," he breathed.

"Hello, Hypnos."

He grabbed her hand in his. "I never thought I'd ever see you again."

"No, I suppose you wouldn't."

He raised a hand and cupped her hollow cheek. "If I had known what she would do…how did you get out?"

"I brought her home," I informed, moving closer to him, making his little creatures squawk and hiss at me as I did. "I found her in oblivion when your mother snapped me there and I got us out."

His attention turned toward me. "Now, I guess you want something from me." He gestured to the others who were just on the edge of sleep, where I'd been. "You summoned me for a purpose."

"Yup, I want you to sneak us into the temple."

"No way. Not happening."

"Your mother is up to something. Something bad, but I'm sure you already know that."

Without answering, Hypnos sighed, slumping onto one of the stone benches. He reached into his pocket and slid out a joint—lighting it with his Zippo lighter that had a bunch of Zzzz's on it. "I don't want to be involved."

"You are already involved."

"What did my idiot brother say to you?"

"He didn't really say anything definitive, but your response just confirmed it for me."

Letting out a heavy breath, he took another hit. "Fine. I don't know if I can get you inside, but I can get you close, but then you are on your own." He stood, pinched off the end and tucked the joint back into his robe, walking over to Hecate. "I've missed you."

"I've missed you too."

Taking her hand in his, he brought it up to where his face should've been, and kissed it. Although, I wasn't sure how he could without lips, but by the look on Hecate's face, he did just that.

"Will there ever be another chance for us?" he asked her.

"Help Melany in any way you can, help her friends, and maybe we can talk about it."

Nodding, his gaze returned to me. "Okay, lie back down and go to sleep. My buddies here will do the rest."

At the mention of his buddies, one of the creatures made a strange chattering noise. I realized it was laughing. That didn't make me feel very confident about its ability to help me do anything, but I had to trust Hypnos. There was no other way into the temple. Nyx would certainly hear us if we went through the portal that Tisiphone and I used. I didn't want to risk climbing the staircase of stars with the possibility of being thrown off them.

I lay back down between Jasmine and Lucian, closing my eyes. Once Hecate waved the burning juniper over my face, I instantly fell back into a drugged state. Consciousness slowly left my mind, letting Hypnos do his job. The sound of fingers snapping reached me, and then I tumbled into sleep.

At first, there was just darkness, but soon I could see a pinpoint of light growing with each second, until I was in an empty white space. Lucian, Jasmine, and Cassandra were there too, looking about as confused as I felt.

Lucian lifted a hand in front of his face. "Is this real? Where are we?"

"We should be going into the dreamworld. Hypnos promised he'd take us to the Temple of Night."

The sound of flapping wings and chattering teeth swiftly filled the white space, and we all whipped around, looking for the source. I knew what it was that was coming, but it still didn't prepare me for the deluge of demonic-looking creatures swarming in our direction and trying to seize us. The others started to fight against the tiny clawed hands.

"Don't! Let them grab you," I shouted.

"What are they?" Jasmine grimaced as two of them pulled at her hair.

"Oneiroi. They're dream creatures. They'll be taking us to the temple."

One by one, we were all lifted into the air by the winged beings holding onto our hair, clothes, and hands. It was definitely uncomfortable in more ways than one, but it had to be done. We were flown out of the empty space and into a dark place that twinkled with stars. It was actually quite beautiful. The pinpoints of light started to change colors. From white to purple, then blue, and all the hues of the rainbow until we were zooming through, all the colors exploding around us like fireworks.

It all abruptly stopped, making my stomach feel like it had rushed up to my throat, and we were dropped onto a black spot of grass on the edge of a cliff. When I got to my feet I could see Nyx's temple in the distance. We were in the sky realm. Hypnos did it.

"Now what?" Lucian asked.

"Now we find the Fates. They're here somewhere. I'm pretty sure that Hypnos put them to sleep, and that's why everything is so messed up. Thanatos mentioned something when I saw him. He probably didn't mean to, but who knows? Death is funny that way."

"You're the only one who's been here before, where do we go?" Lucian gestured to the night realm.

"Let's try the garden first."

I led them across the plain of black grass and violet bushes. Everything here was as dark as the Goddess herself. As we approached the garden, I slowed my steps, my gaze flittering from one area to the next. The last thing we needed was to be ambushed by Nyx and snapped out of existence. We had to find the Fates, wake them up before

Hera could get here and force them to rethread Zeus's lifeline.

My hand instictevely brushed over my pocket, where I kept Hades's thread. It was a reminder to give me strength for what I had to do.

Soon. Soon we'll be together.

Continuing to walk while the others followed close behind me, we came to a stone archway that was the entrance to the oasis.

"What are we looking for exactly?" Jasmine whispered.

"I guess we'll know when we see it."

I motioned for them to enter, and we all came into the garden searching the grounds for three sleeping Fates, which we didn't find.

"They must be in the temple." I gestured to the imposing gothic castle made of black marble.

"What's the play here?" Lucian asked. "What do we do when we find them?"

"Wake them up. Then everything should realign itself, and Zeus will stay dead with no chance to be resurrected." I shrugged. "At least I hope that's what happens."

"And no chance of resurrecting me, darling…"

His voice whispered in my ears, making me shiver.

"I know. That's not the plan anymore."

Darting out of the wooded enclosure, we made our way up the large stone steps to the temple, and to the closed double doors. It was the not the way I had come before. I tried the handles, the doors were locked. "Shit."

Georgina was alongside me. "Let me try." Her metal hand curled around one of the handles and squeezed. It disintegrated in her vice grip, until she was able to push the door open with ease.

We all went inside, careful to make as little noise as possible, but it was difficult as the entire realm had a heady silence to it. The stillness was cloying and actually brushed against my skin like dew drops, so every step inside sounded like a loud thud to my ears.

I didn't know what to expect from this entrance into the temple, but it soon became apparent that it was just one big throne room, with no other notice-able rooms inside it. We ended up in the same hall where I'd first seen Nyx sitting on her black throne, blending into the stone itself. As far as I could tell, we were alone right now.

"There's no one here," Lucian murmured. "Maybe we should just leave before it's too late."

Glancing around me, I was almost inclined to

agree, but Thanatos had more or less told me the Fates were here. Where were they?

I was about to suggest that we take another tour of the grounds, when Cassandra dropped to the floor and started to seize. We all crouched next to her, cautious and concerned, Jasmine held her head so it didn't bounce on the harsh ground, and waited as she had her vision.

After a few minutes, Cassandra stopped moving, then she slowly blinked open her eyes. Lucian helped her sit up gently.

"Are you okay?"

Slowly, she nodded, but her gaze came to land on me. The way she regarded me told me all I needed to know about what her vision had revealed. I wrapped my arms around her, pulling her into a hug.

"Don't tell them. Please don't tell them," I whispered into her ear.

When I leaned back and looked her in the eyes, she gave me a nod, and I breathed a sigh of relief.

Unfortunately, that was short lived.

A raspy chuckle came from the dais behind us the next second, and we all turned to see the shadows undulating. Nyx, the Goddess of Night, materialized.

CHAPTER EIGHTEEN

MELANY

I jumped to my feet. The others did too; Lucian wrapped an arm around Cassandra who was still shaking from her vision. The Goddess of Night was both glorious and terrible to behold. You didn't want to look at her, but also couldn't turn away. Her skin was as black as ink as were her clothes, so the only things you could see were her star-lit eyes, and the crescent moon on her forehead. Yet, there was no mistaking the two robed figures on either side of her. Thanatos and Hypnos, her sons.

"Nice to see you again, Nyx," I greeted sarcastically.

Her star eyes flashed on and off as she blinked. "There's nothing nice about seeing you again, Melany. You're a giant pain in the ass to be honest."

"Ouch. That almost hurt my feelings."

"I underestimated your tenacity. I never thought you'd find a way out of oblivion."

"I had help."

She walked down the steps of the dais, nodding. "Hecate. I'd almost forgotten she even existed."

"She hasn't forgotten you or what you've done."

"Ah, so that's how you got here." She turned to, I assume, glare at Hypnos. "She still has a hold on my son, I see."

"That must suck, having your son betray you."

She chuckled again, and it sent another shiver down my back. "Not all my sons are betrayers."

The sound of scuttling and chattering filled the hall until we were surrounded by fifty Oneiroi. One of them flew to her, landing on her outstretched hand. She brought it to her face and nuzzled it, making kissy sounds.

"Gross," Jasmine murmured under her breath and we shared a look, shudering.

When the Goddess waved her hand, the little

demonic creatures flew toward us, grabbing at our hair and clothes. They were trying to restrain us. I smacked one away, but another took its place. Jasmine and I both tried to use our fire power, but it wasn't effective.

I pulled my lightning to the surface, electrifying my skin, but it didn't do much either. It was like the little jolts of electricity were tickling their little hands. They made weird giggling noises, then just grab me again.

"They're dream creatures, they're not based in reality. None of your powers will work against them." Nyx cackled, and it was like sandpaper being scratched together.

While we struggled against them, knocking one away after another, there seemed to be more streaming in like cockroaches—cat-sized, bat-like winged cockroaches with tiny pointed teeth and beady red eyes.

Lucian tried to get his wings out so he could fight them in the air, but they swarmed all over his wings, making them and him immobile. Eventually, so many of them piled on him, that they forced him, face first, onto the stone floor. More came and we all ended up trapped, and unable to move.

When the far door of the hall opened, Hera,

followed by Apollo, entered. As they drew closer I saw that Apollo carried the old wooden spinning wheel from the Cave of Memory. I thought I'd broken it, but obviously it had been repaired. Or maybe it couldn't ever be completely destroyed.

Hera's gaze flickered over to us. "I see you handled that problem, finally."

"How was I to know that she was clever enough to escape oblivion."

"Yes, she is proving to be a lot smarter than I gave her credit for."

Hera and Apollo stood at the base of the dais. Apollo set the wheel down on the ground.

"Shall we get this over with?" Hera asked, gesturing to the wheel.

"Of course." Nyx nodded to Hypnos, and he raised his hand in the air, slowly lowering it.

At first, I didn't understand what he was doing, but then I saw the Fates suspended mid-air, eyes closed as if they were asleep, floating down from the cathedral ceiling.

"I don't get why you're doing this, Nyx," I called out to her. "It doesn't make any sense."

She came down the remaining steps and approached me. "Because I want more. I'm tired of staying in the sky. I want to spread my darkness. I want a piece of the mortal realm."

"And you think Zeus will grant you that power?"

She didn't say anything, so I assumed that was what she thought.

"There's no way Zeus will share power with you. If Hera promised you that, she's lying. Zeus doesn't share power with anyone."

"He shared it with Hades." Her eyes flashed toward me again. "And with him gone, there's room for a new mistress of the dark."

"Yeah, me."

Laughter escaped her, echoing on the room loudly. I had to grit my teeth to bear it. "Oh, child, you are delusional. I love it. It'll make all of this so much more gratifying." The Goddess turned back around and moved toward the Fates, who hovered five feet above the floor.

"Wake them," she demanded of her son.

Hypnos's hand touched each of the robed women on the forehead, just below their crowns made of thorns. One by one they woke, and were set back onto their feet.

Hera handed Zeus's severed thread to Clothos. "Reweave it."

Taking the golden lifeline, the Fate padded over to the spinning wheel. Her fingers ran over its wooden curves like a man caressing a woman's skin. Reaching into her robe, she took out a spindle of golden thread and set it over the stick at the top of the wheel. Slowly, she bent to sit, and a stool magically appeared beneath her backside.

Ironically, I fell mesmerized by the Fate's actions, as she used her foot to get the wheel spinning. We were witnessing the design of a life. The moment where the soul was created and weaved into a golden piece of silk. When I looked over at the others, they each had similar looks of awe on their faces.

Clothos took Zeus's old thread and wrapped it around a new piece of silk, but it wouldn't stay. It kept unthreading, as if it knew it wasn't meant to become whole.

"What's happening?" Hera demanded. "Why isn't it working?"

Clothos's head tilted toward Hera. Her features covered by her veil so I couldn't see if she was actually looking at the Goddess. "To weave this again, we need blood."

Hera held out her hand. "Take it from me."

The Fate's head slowly shook. "It must be from

a hero."

My heart leapt into my throat, and I turned to look at Lucian on the ground. As our gazes met, I felt the whole world fall out from under me.

Apollo stepped forward. "Take mine."

"You are not pure of heart and soul."

Seething, Hera looked over at Lucian as well, pointing a condemning finger his way. "Bring him."

The Oneiroi picked him up and dragged him over to Hera.

"NO!" I shoved at the little creatures, trying not only to move, but to get my hands free.

Jasmine, Georgina and Cassandra all shouted with me, struggling against their restraints. As soon as Lucian was close enough, Hera withdrew a dagger from her belt, setting it to his throat.

"Take me instead!" I screamed. "Exchange my life for his."

Surprised, Hera, lowered the blade, glancing over at Clothos. "Can this be done?"

The Fate turned her head toward me, then nodded. "Yes, she is of pure heart and soul. She will satisfy the requirements."

Despite the circumstances, relief surged through me to hear that. Deep inside I worried that my heart was now as dark as Nyx's, and my soul had become as corrupted as Hera's.

As the creatures dragged me forward, they took Lucian back to where the others were while he kicked and roared.

"Don't do this!" Lucian begged.

My eyes went to him, seeing the young man I'd fallen for the night he pulled me out of the water. The beautiful generous soul of a hero. My love for him would always exist. Nothing could destroy it. Not even death.

Screaming, Jasmine and Georgina struggled against the hold the Oneiroi had on the them. I loved them for it. I loved the fight and heart of each of my soul sisters. I'd never find two stronger, or more compassionate warriors.

Cassandra just stared at me. She'd known this was coming. She'd seen it in her vision. Yet, I nodded to her reasuringly.

"Remember, there wouldn't be darkness without light!" I shouted.

"Blue!" Lucian raged. "Fight them!"

A smile curved my lips as I held his gaze, and Hera pressed her dagger against my throat. "Always."

Before she could slice open my neck, I looked

over her shoulder at Thanatos who still stood unflinching on the dais.

"Do it!" My eyes snapped to Hypnos. "Keep your promise to Hecate!"

Thanatos snapped his fingers, fulfilling the deal we'd made, just as a second snap echoed in the room. Satisfaction coursed through me, knowing my friends would be safe.

I closed my eyes against the swell of the brightest light I'd ever experienced.

CHAPTER NINETEEN

LUCIAN

*W*ith a snap of Thanatos's deadly fingers, Melany vanished from sight.

One second she was there, Hera's knife cutting into her throat, the next she was gone. Poof, disappeared.

"Nooo!" I broke away from the little demons' clutches, or they let go, I wasn't sure, and ran toward her. I was too late though. Melany was already gone.

Screams erupted from Hera too, but for very different reasons.

Hypnos' had snapped his fingers as well, and a light as powerful as the sun pressed down on her, Apollo, and Nyx instantly. Hera dropped to her knees, arms flying to her face to block the brightness, but it wasn't enough to combat the power of it. Soon, her skin started to blacken and crack like a piece of chicken on the barbeque.

Apollo's eyes closed, his face basking in the harsh glow, except he looked like a golden statue, frozen in place. Nyx's screech split the air, and she suddenly exploded into fragments of black glass. Pieces of her dropped onto the floor, making sharp, tinkling noises like tiny bells ringing.

Shocked, I turned to see the source of the blinding light, my hand lifting to shield my eyes so I wouldn't go blind.

Cassandra floated high above us in the air, eyes glowing white, arms flung out to the sides, while her whole body radiated like a small sun. It was spectacular to witness.

Jasmine and Georgina stood behind her too stunned to move, admiring her from under their hands, mouths agape.

Then the light blinked out of existence, like turning off a light switch, and Cassandra floated down to the ground. I reached her before she could fall over, and wrapped my arm around her. Her body sagged against me, completely exhausted.

"Is it over?" Jasmine asked as she stepped up beside me.

"I think so."

"What about Melany?" Georgina's gaze surveyed the hall.

Releasing a burdened breath, Cassandra shook her head. "She's gone."

"What do you mean gone?" My gut tightened, not wanting to know the answer.

"She's dead." Thanatos and Hypnos floated across the hall to hover in front of us. They were twins in black robes and nothingness under the hood, except thick black space.

"Melany made a deal with me over your friend's life." He nodded to Jasmine, and I realized he meant Mia. "She promised to surrender her soul to me, on a time of her choosing, if it would save you. All of you. And I accepted."

Tears rolled down Jasmine's cheeks instantly, her head falling. "Oh, Mel," she whispered as Georgina pulled her into a hug. Their sobs pierced me right in the heart and I couldn't catch my breath.

The room shifted under my feet with the revelation, and I doubled over, trying to take in air.

But it wouldn't come. My chest constricted so tightly, gripping me like a vice, and I was certain I'd never breathe again. I wasn't sure I even wanted to.

Melany was gone.

How could I face that?

A hand rested on my back, and I twisted around to see Cassandra rubbing it slowly, trying to soothe me. Surprisingly it did.

"I will take you back to the academy," Hypnos offered.

"What about the Fates?" I peered over to where they'd been standing, to find that they were gone.

"Back where they belong," Thanatos offered. "In the Cave of Memory. Weaving, allotting, and cutting the threads of life."

"So, everything will be back to normal?" I questioned, although right now I wasn't really sure what normal meant.

Thanatos nodded. "Yes. People will be born, they will live, and they will die..."

As promised, Hypnos returned us to the academy, back to the middle of the maze where we'd first gone to sleep. Hecate was there, sitting on the grass just as we'd left her, waiting. When she saw Hypnos, she went to him and they embraced.

Turning toward us, she walked to my side and gently cupped my cheek. "Melany was a beautiful dark soul, and she will be missed." Hecate moved over to Jasmine, Georgina, and then Cassandra, doing the same. "But she's left pieces in each of you. Embrace them."

We left the maze and returned to the academy. It was still night so when we walked through the front doors, there was no one there waiting for us. There was no welcome community, or greeting, no fanfare for a heroes' return. Once again, no one would know what Melany had done to save them, to save the world. What she had sacrificed for all of them. For us. For me.

The halls were dark and empty as we walked them to get to the infirmary.

Mia and Ren were both awake, and sitting up in their beds when we entered. It was as if they knew that something horrible had happened, and were waiting for us to return to share it with them.

I did. I told them what had happened.

Jasmine went to Mia when she started to sob uncontrollably. She sat on the bed pulling her into her arms and rocked her.

Ren reached for my hand, and I sat in the chair beside his bed, allowing him to hug me. "I'm so sorry Lucian."

I didn't know what to say. There were words to express the pure heartbreak and misery I felt, so I didn't say anything. I just sat there, numb, and let Ren cry for his friend, for my Blue, on my shoulder until he was empty...

SIX MONTHS LATER

I dove into the pool of water that lead toward the portal to the mortal realm. Ren dove in next to me with Cassandra after him. Jasmine, Mia, and the others had already gone ahead of us. After I climbed out onto pier nine, dried off my body, I shook out my wings and shot to the sky. It took only about ten minutes to fly from Cala to Pecunia.

The newly reconstructed town square, hummed with activity as I landed among my friends and peers in the park, in front of the erected stage. The place was filled with people from all over the area. I nodded to Hephaistos and Heracles, who stood among the buzzing crowd, waiting for the big unveiling. The family Melany used to live with, Callie Demos and her mother, Mrs. Demos, stood in the audience close to the stage.

Mayor Remis climbed the few stairs up, and stood at the microphone, tapping it once to check it was on. It made a loud thumping noise that echoed through the park. He laughed. "Just checking."

A few reciprocal chuckles came from the crowd.

"Welcome, everyone! I'm so glad to see so many people here to celebrate this glorious day!"

That got some cheers.

"Not that long ago we were here to unveil the new Pecunia Victory Mall, that we'd built from the ashes after the Battle of the Gods. Many of the Gods and heroes from that battle were here to help us celebrate that moment. Six months ago, we once again faced great adversity and those same Gods and heroes came to our defense once more." He waved his hand toward the part of the crowd where I and many others stood. "Today, we are here to celebrate one such hero, who sacrificed everything to save us once again."

Prometheus climbed the stairs, inciting a few gasps came from the townspeople, who had never seen a seven-foot tall Titan in a white robe before.

Prometheus stood in front of the microphone, bending down to speak into it.

"Hello. My name is Prometheus and I'm the head of the Demigods Academy. I'm here today to tell you about a special young woman, who altered my life and the lives of many here today. I would still be locked away in Tartarus if it hadn't been for her, and her fiercely loyal friends, who are also here with us."

With his words, I swallowed down the well of emotion rising in my chest. A hand suddenly slid into mine, briefly startling me, but I looked over to see Cassandra standing next to me. That warm and calming smile that always made me feel better curved her lips, working its magic on me once more.

"Melany Richmond was the feistiest, most rebellious young woman I ever had the pleasure of instructing," Prometheus continued.

I chuckled, as did Jasmine and Georgina, who stood nearby.

"She was strong, skilled, smart, astute, and stubborn. I'd once called her reckless and careless, but now I realized that she cared. She cared more than anyone I'd ever known. And because of that fierce devotion to others, she made the greatest sacrifice a hero can make to save the people, and a world that didn't even know it needed saving."

I knew Melany would get a kick out of this if she could hear it. Prometheus, singing her praises for all the world to hear, was a sight to behold.

"Today, I have the pleasure of unveiling a tribute to Melany. A tribute to the greatest hero the academy has ever produced." He waved a hand toward the giant tarp that covered the ten foot tall structure, and it was pulled away.

As the fabric fell, a statue of Melany was revealed in all her glory.

A collective gasp of awe went through the crowd and everyone clapped.

Hephaistos had outdone himself. The crafts-manship on the dark stone was unrivaled.

Melany stood on the pedestal, her giant black wings extended to their full width. She was dressed in her battle gear, and wore those big black boots that were made to kick ass. In one hand she held her shield up to her chest for protection—the actual shield she made in Hephaistos's forging class. In the other, she lifted her sword up in front of her face, an invitation to battle.

The look he had etched on her face was perfect. It was a combination of snark and determination.

Like she always knew a joke you didn't. On her head, Hephaistos set the helm of darkness that Hades had him make for her, and at the base of her feet lay a plague that read:

"Melany "Blue" Richmond, The Dark Angel of Pecunia."

She looked exactly how I would always see her. Fierce, protective, and beautiful. A true dark angel.

"It's beautiful," Cassandra whispered.

"It is." I squeezed her hand.

Georgina bounced in beside us. "I'm starving. Do you guys want to get some pancakes?"

"Yeah, that sounds perfect."

Cassandra, Jasmine, Mia, Ren and Georgina, and I, all walked along the park to the little strip mall across the street. There was a new breakfast place that recently opened called *Melany's Pancakes*. Although he'd never admit it, I knew that Dionysus had a hand in opening it up.

It was a perfect kind of day. Plenty of sunshine, birds chirping, kids running around playing, and a gorgeous blue sky, the same color as Mel's hair.

EPILOGUE

MELANY

*S*lowly, I opened my eyes and stared up at the maroon curtains of the canopy surrounding my giant bed. My head to look at the empty spot on the bed beside me. Of course it was empty. It always was when I awoke.

I sat up and swung my legs over the mattress, to settle my feet into the furry slippers I kept there. Standing, I adjusted the long, black silky nightie I wore. Too long in my opinion. If it had been my choice alone I would've worn a t-shirt and boxer shorts to bed.

It was a bit cold in the room, so I grabbed the

matching robe that had been draped over the chair, and slipped it on, tying it tightly at my waist. I left the room, and tiptoed down the wide dark corridor, the firelight glowing from the juncture of the wall and floor lighting my way to the last door on the right.

Entering the room, I plunked down in one of the high-backed ornate chairs. There was a cup of steaming hot coffee on the mahogany table with my name on it. Literally. The coffee mug said, MELANY, in big bold red letters. I took a sip of the coffee, heavy on the sugar and cream, and sighed contentedly. My gaze fell on my companion, who was staring at me expectantly, with a cup of tea in his hand and an arch to his wonderfully sculpted eyebrow.

"Good morning," I cooed.

"Finally. You're up. You sleep too much," Hades mused, penetrating eyes on me.

"It only seems like I sleep too much because you don't sleep at all." I plucked a ripe strawberry from his plate and popped it into my mouth, the juice ran down my chin and he shook his head.

"You could use a napkin. It wouldn't kill you."

"It might." Lips curling, I picked up the folded black cotton napkin on the table, and wiped my face to appease him. Hades could be so grumpy in the mornings. Or afternoons, since I didn't know which was when. Time didn't really exist here, and that was perfectly fine with me.

When Thanatos snapped his fingers, claiming my life, Hypnos had snapped his too and sent me here. After all these months, I still wasn't sure if it was real or a dream. I didn't really care either way. I was where I wanted to be. Where I had always been fated to be.

"What do you want to do today?" I snatched another strawberry from his plate before he could grab my hand.

That sexy eyebrow went up again. "We could go back to that bed you seem so fond of."

My cheeks warmed instantly. He had a fabulously gifted way of making me blush all the time. Even now. After all this time.

"Can we go to Mardi Gras? I've never been. And it looks like way too much fun."

I tried to snatch more fruit, but he caught my hand, bringing it up to his mouth to press his lips onto the back. A rush of heat surged up my arm. "Sounds perfect, my dear. I do love a chance to dress up."

Hades slid his plate across the table to me. "If

you're hungry, I could ask Charon to make you pancakes if you like."

"I'm good. I don't really have a craving for pancakes right now." Standing, I sat on his lap, straddling him in his chair.

His hands immediately cupped my ass. "What are you craving then?"

"Just you, my love."

I leaned forward and pressed my lips to his.

AUTHORS' NOTE:

Thanks for reading the Demigods Academy series. If you loved Melany's story, consider leaving a review on Amazon. Just one or two lines would be very helpful to support us.

Hugs,

Elisa & Kiera

ABOUT THE AUTHORS

Elisa S. Amore is the number-one bestselling author of the paranormal romance saga *Touched*.

Vanity Fair Italy called her "the undisputed queen of romantic fantasy." After the success of Touched, she produced the audio version of the saga featuring Hollywood star Matt Lanter (*90210, Timeless, Star Wars*) and Disney actress Emma Galvin, narrator of *Twilight* and *Divergent*. Elisa is now a full-time writer of young adult fantasy. She's wild about pizza and also loves traveling, which she calls a source of constant inspiration. With her successful series about life and death, Heaven and Hell, she has built a loyal fanbase on social media that continues to grow, and has quickly become a favorite author for thousands of readers in the U.S.

Visit Elisa S. Amore's website and join her List of Readers at www.ElisaSAmore.com and Text AMORE to 77948 for new release alerts.

FOLLOW ELISA S. AMORE:

facebook.com/eli.amore

instagram.com/eli.amore

twitter.com/ElisaSAmore

elisa.amore@touchedsaga.com

***

Kiera Legend writes Urban Fantasy and Paranormal Romance stories that bite. She loves books, movies and Tv-Shows. Her best friends are usually vampires, witches, werewolves and angels. She never hangs out without her little dragon. She especially likes writing kick-ass heroines and strong world-buildings and is excited for all the books that are coming!

Text LEGEND to 77948 to don't miss any of them (US only) or sign up at www.kieralegend.com to get an email alert when her next book is out.

FOLLOW KIERA LEGEND:

facebook.com/groups/kieralegend

facebook.com/kieralegend

authorkieralegend@gmail.com

Made in the USA
Las Vegas, NV
13 June 2021